The Plotline Bomber of Innisfree

The Plotline Bomber of Innisfree

•

Josh Massey

BOOKTHUG
DEPARTMENT OF NARRATIVE STUDIES
TORONTO, 2015

FIRST EDITION

The production of this book was made possible through the generous assistance of the Canada Council for the Arts and the Ontario Arts Council. BookThug also acknowledges the support of the Government of Canada through the Canada Book Fund and the Government of Ontario through the Ontario Book Publishing Tax Credit and the Ontario Book Fund.

 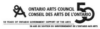

LIBRARY AND ARCHIVES CANADA CATALOGUING IN PUBLICATION

Massey, Josh, 1979-, author
    The plotline bomber of Innisfree / Josh Massey.

Issued in print and electronic formats.
ISBN 978-1-77166-126-3 (paperback).--ISBN 978-1-77166-127-0 (html).--ISBN 978-1-77166-128-7 (pdf).--ISBN 978-1-77166-129-4 (mobi kindle)

    I. Title.

PS8626.A7989P56 2015   C813'.6   C2015-905697-7
                                           C2015-905698-5

PRINTED IN CANADA

A **bundled** eBook edition is available with the purchase of this print book.

CLEARLY PRINT YOUR NAME ABOVE IN UPPER CASE

Instructions to claim your eBook edition:
1. Download the Shelfie app for Android or iOS
2. Write your name in **UPPER CASE** above
3. Use the Shelfie app to submit a photo
4. Download your eBook to any device

Tonight and forever the Wapiti move thru
water hemlock
and bend their necks into the soil of the lower plains.
—Ebbe Borregaard, 1957

Pipeline Controversy Erupts

—1 September 2036—

The Can'tadian State Department has sanctioned stage three in Pipe Nexus expansion. The collective announcement came today from the parlepasliamentary committee assessing the project.

"It was a difficult decision, but we believe in the case of this particular Gasbro pipeline that the dangers are outweighed by the necessity of increased ethical flow to foreign markets," said today's committee report.

The decision comes in the wake of a one million litre spill from an older Gasbro wooden pipeline on the Squashington border which officials say is being mopped.

The third major east-to-west project of its kind since the 2006 Pan-Phallus Extender, Pipe Nexus 3 will run 1,600 kilometres from the province of Cowberta though PC Columbia on its way to tanker docks in the testy river valleys of the northwestern coast.

Gasbro's goal is to facilitate transport of bitumenlite to the rapidly expanded Wenese/Can'tadian Processing Alliance Outlet overseas and the South Polar Civilization Initiative. Pipe Nexus 3 is a supposed advancement in high-pressure transport, and the new three-ply pipes are capable of transporting quintuple the bitumenlite as traditional conduits: approximately two million barrels a day. The $20 billion project – which never received major opposition due to a media hush and protest chill – could commence construction as early as May, 2037.

Opponent Jim Rutherford of Animal Alliance has called the proposed pipeline "an idiot attempt to trapeze through one of the most treacherous and fragile environments on the planet and birth canals of the oceans' salmon supply."

Cassandra Jeremiah of *Skeptic City TV*, on the other hand, calls the project a necessary step towards avoiding a tenth consecutive recession: "We are, in this day and age, capable of performing these operations much less invasively. There is no reason why human technology and the green world cannot merge through integrated systems cooperation."

Visit *Troutsource* frequently over the days and months ahead for the latest developments in what's sure to be yet another dramatic story about development and those who oppose it. As an independent news source, "we release the gag and let silenced tongues wag."

o

In the district county of Enderbee, farther into the mountain corridors than the town of Byzantium and farther than media can go, on my thousand-acre elk ranch called Innisfree—that's where you will find me, Jeffery Inkster, with the elk I serve and the elk who serve me.

Mnemosyne I and Hyperion I were the first animal settlers in this part of Enderbee. Me, the first human settler, I am the humble elk servant with alfalfa feed. All I ask of the elk is their velvet antlers, and all they want from me is food, a fair ration of freedom, and the worship they deserve.

The animal tourists always want to know about predation on elk and elk mating practices. They want to know, for instance, how a Hyperion licks a Mnemosyne from croup to withers before mounting. I like to tell the animal tourists that elks know much more about foreplay than most peoples. As for predation, well, that will most likely come up later on in this tour.

o

Locals started calling me Mr. Happy Man, and coming to the farm. Now I give tours, plant the bean rows, sit on the steps of my newly finished porch, and I tell visitors about processes involving the land. Such as the powers of controlled daydream, how someone can nap before they go down to the secret river of our property, and imagine fish tails forming a doily pattern as they doze. Of course they'll never know who's going to catch the three-spined stickleback when they wake up and go down to that river, but they will know where to place the silver spoon when they dine with the antlered Titans.

Imagine an elk, I might say, who dolphin-leaps over the counter at an emerald-hued café. You can tell by the falling-human-shaped velvet antlers of a second elk beside the soda machine that things are a certain way, that somebody like me, who was born in a wet, readerly city in the lower Northwest, can land in a rancher's life.

Some people have a harder time with the imagining; others find more difficulty in the doing. But at Innisfree ranch those actions are one, which is a beautiful, beautiful thing to see.

o

During the halfway break of this most recent tour, the first week of the season, two kids came running through the pines, gripping a sizeable elk rack, each by a tine. When they saw the rest of the group waiting by the wagon, they did a one-handed bugle—bugling being one of the lessons we teach on the wagon tour. The antlers that weren't harvested for velvet, and that aren't gnawed through by mice, show up as lucky finds on the spring tours. I showed the kids where to fit the rack on a big hive of antlers in the middle of the fence out the main dirt road. Other antlers—there are more than we know what to do with—stick from each post around the forest and river and field. The alfalfa tractor has also got antlers above its grille.

The sun has spirals of laughing youth twirling off its centre, with a proud Elkhead in the middle, or so you can imagine. The elk bugle louder and the children scream songs of play with the same increasing solar urgency. The sun is so strong, even here in the North. The porch gets nuked when there isn't enough venting between the mountains. Don't know how many times I've had to re-finish it.

o

Artists and inventors, fleeing demons or pursuing angels, have found a home in Enderbee County. Like my neighbour Memily, who's an abstract expressionist painter, and grows lettuce in the summer, then blanches that along with other plants for the winter reserves. Talking to her, you will fall into colour, into all the colours of her garden and art, the landscape colours of her eyes. With her husband, Dan-the-Man, she makes art instead of kids, what they call industrial art, which has recently taken a political turn. Take, for instance, the escape capsule, called "The Mattson Rocket," that looks like an old, compact rocket ship out back of their converted storehouse home. It's got steel runners and circular windows, stripes of old machine red over top of the riveted white. And an antenna sticking up from the tip. A nostalgic 2001 look. Memily and her partner built the capsule just in case there is no land left after all the development—a pod to save them, to take off into the skyahhh.

Sure, there are divisions, cliques, and tokenisms, and all that stuffy stuff of small populations in the rough, but, beyond that, the bonds are tight, and we help each other out. Like Memily will come round up the elk with me, and I will irrigate her garden when her and Dan-the-Man go south during asparagus season. Memily will trade her blanched crops for some of the jarred fish that the First Nations bring; I'll share alfalfa and hay. Based on barter, we've gotten along really well here.

I guess we all thought we really knew each other in

Enderbee. But one of us in the community is really good at keeping a secret, and secrets might one day blow our bonds apart.

o

Like what happened just the other day. You see, we hadn't ventured into the big town of Byzantium for some time because—and I can only speak for myself in saying—we were all creaky elbowed and sore hipped from getting ready for the spring elk wagon tours. But finally we got the gumption to drive our little European truck to town. It's always very pleasurable, after weeks in the fields, to enjoy sweets and be bug free. Checking in at the community centre, we were happy to see how many folks had signed up for the wagon tours. I always tell families, if you're looking for an adventuresome excursion, give us a dingle at old Inkster's farm.

It's all the workers moving to the mountain cusps for the projects, and those who are here because of the buzz of what is coming. It is them who want to explore the pioneer cabins, and it is them with the money who fuel this goodly elk enterprise, isn't that right, Artsy Boy?

But this day, what day? . . . no matter . . . this one day when the apple blossoms are fluttering with camouflage butterflies, a guy with tighty-whitey shirt comes up and says: Well, have you heard about this?

He was much fussed up, and he showed me and Samson—our Artsy Boy—some photos of a poster on his phone. Posters that somebody had stuck up around town.

To Can'tadians Who Still Have Time in Their Busy Schedules to Read:
National park is not enough to stop this pipeline.

The pipe which keeps going, the pipe which goes through
and around and through and around.
Jagged mountain, Fanged gorge.
I am called Hypnotist. They came after my poetry too.
But your plan, I wrote of it long before you came.
You will meet me later in the Narrative.
  Your name is Skull Crusher. You will find yourself later in
  the Narrative Wilderness.

If only they knew the underpinnings of their sorry nature.
This is where the imported spooks meet the indigenous
dreams.

Well, Jiminy Cricket, I said, after reading the weird posting. The man showing it to me had no piercings, no tattoos, and was white as new underwear.

The hypnotist mentioned on the poster, I told him, it could be that I remember him. He came creeping around these parts before, many calendars back. He used a chunk of copper from the Charybdis mine on a silver string to make the audience doze, then to suggest stuff that had to do with folks finding a purpose in life. He used music that was of the old country to woo those who came to his shows.

I relocated here with my family to get away from the crazies, said Tighty-Whitey in a husky, sputtering voice.

Said he saw crossdressers here too. Which he thought was only in cities.

His co-worker in the Happy Mines company truck rolled up with a crunching noise, and the guy I was talking with, who had biceps like vanilla ice-cream scoops, told him just a sec, then thumb-tapped the extra large buttons on his phone to show me something else. You know, nice northern town, right. Well, look at this! Are you kidding me?

o

Camp workers like that guy get all watery-eyed when a sad song's played about the old pioneering days. The workers' sadness is all the more so with the huge downpours that came at this year's festival and rinsed people away almost literarily.

Not sure we will have it so close to the river next year on account of the flooding that made for a good story, but not for a good time. The flood caused by the tears of county songs.

Let me tell you about the festival. Actually, let Samson tell you about it.

What Samson, Artsy Boy, great egg begetter, said about this year's event: Talk about a rainy felksival! We were up to our nipples in flood water out at Innisfree! The drum kit floated away, and you had to paddle to get to the food vendors. Had to unplug and go all acoustic, needless to say. People dubbed it Floodstock. It was not cool.

o

Yup, people with problems come to Innisfree. Don't
know where I got all my wisdom, but it's a sought-after
resource, it sure is, and I reckon the magic's in the antlers. Visitors sit on my porch and I play for them a number on my hurdy-gurdy, which is pretty much a fiddle in
a box with a handle that, when rotated, cranks the bow
over the strings.

There are times when winds fall what appear to be the
sturdiest trees, times when the roses shake with wasps,
times when the leaves and dust spin up in whirligigs of
grit. Despite the day's condition, and no matter how de-
pressing the big trucks with their demonmachine head-
light glare and grinning grille, the galvanized egos, and
the destroyed land, I will always tell the visitors through
my thorny white beard *Just try to just keep lovin'*. Keep
lovin' all da time. It's the only song I ever wrote for the
gurdy, in fact. Called it "Keep Lovin' All Da Time." Turn
the crank in the box and crank out the song of love like
ore. I'm not sure what it does for all their problems, but
I keep playing it.

When I crank the gurdy, a Mnemosyne will come trot-
ting to the porch with her bib of ratty chest hair wet from
the pond. The horns of a Hyperion turn in the daddy elk
pen, and the globes on his forehead absorb me. I brush
my fingers through brown fur. Feel wet hair rub against
my shoulder. Healing to touch the elk like that, and to
smell the beastliness of their fur.

19

Gasbro Reaches Out To Bomber

—12 October 2036—

A leak sprung from a major Gasbro natural gas pipeline has been called an act of terrorism by company executive Chase Beefrude in a press release Friday. Beefrude, a major player in Cowbertan Oil Diamond operations, told the scrum of reporters outside the main headquarters in Cancougar that he wishes to negotiate with the individual in order to prevent further situations.

"We want the individual responsible for the bombing to speak to us. It is our hope that we can make a deal with them, and try to understand their concerns," said Beefrude.

Insider Oil Diamond reporter Andrew Coppernickel points out that the timing of the sabotage attempt—with the Gasbro Pipe Nexus 3 bitumenlite high-pressure project recently okayed in Parlepasliament and slated for construction within two years—hints at a potential warning bomb.

"The culture of the bomb is strong," Coppernickel told *Troutsource*. "This most recent blast, far enough from workers not to cause them harm but close enough to instill fear, has all the hallmarks of a strategic warning charge."

Several sources say that bombers are being financed by green angel investors from Lowcalifornia.

The bombing comes a week after an anonymous threat letter was mailed to Gasbro headquarters. The letter detailed several of the bomber's complaints, including "the greedy clown's vanishing tree act," in reference to the Commons area near the border with Cowberta where a self-governing structure exists but which has been sought out by various developers because of its gas and mineral plays.

The violent language of the threat letter has created a wave of fear in the industry, with a temporary halt called on the construction of several lines in the area.

The Byzantium police detachment is offering a reward of $100,000 for any information leading to the arrest of people associated with the recent blasts.

o

Samson asks if I heard what the Carlyle family been up to. Blockading Kelly Rd. Mad as hell about the strangers in their trucks. Bombs and blockades. Shit is going down, he says.

I heave up a wet hay block, which nags my bad shoulder. And the sides of my hands are so itchy, like I wore a horsehair glove or something. Makes me irritated.

Well, so am I, I say. Mad, I mean. These new pipeline crews don't even know how to tie a frigging gate knot when they use our roads. Lost a few head of elk last year. They're turning me into an angry old man!

Samson looks up from his video camera and says: Probably using all the dynamite stolen from Paul Bunion Mill, as an exclamation mark.

What's this about the missing dynamite, Samson?

Heard it on the Internet radio I just installed. TNT from a copper mine.

On Byzantium radio? I never heard that.

Well, it was on the radio, Jeffery. When we were just in town. Damn sure it's the Carlyles who are the ones rattling the Gasbro operations. The Carlyles being the ones with the most know-how around here.

You are an old investigator dog. Young artsy egg farmer like you, hah!

Right on, Inkster, yeah, can solve things just by looking yourself. Like they are trying to pin this on lefties, but what if it's someone pretending to be them, like it's a scheme by someone, by a righty even, trying to snatch the reward money by framing themselves as lefties.

Whoever they are, and they could be righties or lefties or both-way loosies, they're going to do something really really, *really really really really* destructive eventually. Dynamite and nitroglycerine is one thing, but you never know what a fruitnut can get their hands on these days, like that there piric acid or them there Sprengkorpers. Anyway . . . and listen, Samson, I appreciate you helping out extra today. The leaves are yellow and brown, the berries are anger-red, the streams are fearful cold, the geese are vanished in the skyahhh. Have some birch syrup to take back to your feathered palace. You give much of your time as a volunteer ranch hand. And thank you for the eggs.

Thanks, Inkster! And guess what, I just sold all my eggs to a man who came by on his way to Florida. He really likes my special eggs.

Great to hear, Samson. I sold two kilos of elk powder to what must be the same gentleman. And gave him some capsules for the long drive.

Fancy that. Well, until tomorrow then, Inkster.

And what is that redness he has on his neck, by the ears? Something similar on the elk, too.

o

But these issues evolve from the outside, you see, and there's an ocean of peace still within us. So moving on now, you probably want to know something about elk. I know you want to know about the harem system, indeed you do, but what about the hard science of the species first in terms of their classifications? An unspeakable combination of things, the elk is, or what I've read in Artsy Boy's books are called ecotone-loving mammals, belonging to them plant and animal kinds that thrive within hazy green brackets: pasture/forest; pasture/creek; aspen/pine. Those sorts of transition places where representatives of the different areas share ground.

Some on full alert, others sedate (especially on nights I put the sleep licks in their trough). Like all herd animals, elk express their uniqueness by the way they occupy so many different spots in a field, all in different positions. Some licking a hoof, some with moss forked on their antlers to make them look larger. Some presenting profile, others flank, one peeing while another sips from that stream. The wide view of the elk pasture gets quite amusing.

Sometimes coyotes slink down the side of a draw from the uplands in an attempt to get access to the smorgasbord of prey. Reminds of what Mayor Timothy said of the pipeline bombers, that they're like Wile E. Coyotes, sneaking around to bomb the Road Runner. However, despite being strong-legged like a Road Runner, able to kick in a coyote brain or frighten a fox, elks tend to leave their young in frozen hiding positions while they attempt a deer-type distraction.

Elk adaptation was a little wonky, I'd have to say, like when the males grimace and flash their teeth, which would make sense if they still had long teeth like they used to hundreds of thousands of years ago, but it just looks silly in this day and age. To be frank, they look like grinning donkeys when they do that.

Sometimes I think of an elk machine that was made through predator choosing, through disease choosing, and finally through landscape choice: the elkclockmaker called time and the drelkams that are its brood.

Sometimes I lie around with the herd in the wintertime by the shrunken streams and powdered reeds, wearing my snow pants and my down jacket. The elks would choose this life, because at least, though it is a life of bondage, they have an opportunity to breathe the air. And I am not sure they know otherwise. Prey are idealists.

o

Pushing a wheelbarrow full of stones into Innisfree along the side of the road, the guy from the other day pulled up beside me again on his way out to the Happy Mines.

What's up, Tighty-Whitey, I said.

The name's Chuck D, he said, scratching his armpit as he reached out his phone again with his other hand and showed me something. He said it was a letter that somebody mailed to the community paper, and so he'd gone taken a picture of it too.

Dear Gasbro, Heed this warning or else it'll be disappear-in-a-puff-of-smoke time. The Free Bear Alliance is giving you fucks mere weeks to get out of our mountain lands. The damage you will begin witnessing tonight is but a taste of what is to come if you continue building through the title lands of Enderbee. The time has come for this county to once and for all ban all development in the sacred lands overseen by Allies and Firsts. We will not stop forcefully resisting until you are either absent or dead. Have you heard of Meech? In our mountain language this means Skull Crusher. If you do not stop drilling in our land you will be introduced to Meech Accord. We will collapse your skulls in this rock-grinding machine and we will juice your brains and slurp them down in front of your families.

Well, Dag Nabbit, I said. This is more than enough to rouse the sleeping fowl of the fields from their pleasant slumbers.

The man's mouth moved underneath a moustache sharp like the bones of minnows, eyebrows like peppery Velcro, and said: To put it mildly, letters like these make us visitors and newcomers feel more than a wee bit unwelcome.

And then he hopped into his truck and him and his co-worker wheeled off into the scars of the land.

I had a dream later, one of the open-eyed ones you get in the bean rows. I was talking to the same guy.

Hey, Chuck D?

What?

Could you help me out? I got to buy a new cider press, or fix this one for the umpteenth time.

Chuck D scrunched his nose, then reached into the console between the front seats of this truck, grabbed a fistful of bills and tossed them out the window. Sorry about the mess, he said, as the bills scattered on the road around me.

I got on my knees and gathered the money up. Thinking it's all right, because farmers can't be choosers.

o

Yeah, well, you know they've called this "the back-to-work century," which is kind of not what we're all about on Innisfree Ranch, as we prefer leisure labour of a sort. These days wholesalers are buying crop before the seed's even in the ground, and calves before they're even born yet. We all try our hands at small-time farming, but the thing is, the financial risk isn't worth it. You have to invest in the fastest farmbots and supercombines to be able to ensure a yield that will enable you to make ends meet, and you finance it by signing agreements with a buyer for X amount of product predicted on your first year. Instead of giving us boosters, the Can'tadian government made a back-to-work regimen, so farmers ended up having to take positions such as waiter and traffic controller. And the weather got so unreliable that you can't know for certain your future yield. Even the almanac, that Nostradamus-work of wise rural people, is getting it wrong. It takes imagination to do something a little different, to find that niche market, like velvet antler. Or by finding some plant that has medicinal properties, and package it for the mass market under a good name.

o

Well, it all started I don't know when—a while ago, I guess. First it was the flesh-wasting disease that attacked the elks some years ago. Then, well, why does it matter if it was before or after the bombs started? Leaks happen either way and I swear time sort of rises and falls, drifts and billows at Innisfree, like Artsy Boy says, subject to the emanations of the earth and the winds and such. When I washed my hands in the eaves barrels, and splashed the rainwater on my face, it made my eyes get bleary. It was the chemicals pumped up from deep down in the earth—methane, benzene, and the oxides, coming in the fog and condensing in our drinking barrels. Saw Samson through my tears, wiped them off, and tried to act like my jovial self.

What's up, Samson, how did the tour go with the Primrose family? Not good, judging by your expression. Your moustache looks concerned.

The kids noticed something, they did. Back there near the creek.

Noticed what?

Samson leads me through the tails of grass, his heels tensing beneath the rolled bottoms of jeans, through the heavy blue of the day, the spillbottle colours along the horizon . . . There, in a saucer of splayed grass . . . could see a Mnemosyne trying to keep her head high and alert but obviously wilted from some great strain, the antlers like rotating blivets sticking up from the highbush cranberry, turning wearily around in her surveillance mode, not even trusting us at first, trying to scramble away sideways. Followed a cord of flesh coming out of her canal to a dead elk fetus . . . in sight of one of the bitumenlite wells over there.

I cradled that dead calf, all its veins visible through its transparent skin, skull underdeveloped and paper-thin, its hooves dripping down from my arms, and saw Mnemosyne there, helpless with placenta dangling out from her behind—the Roman number XX looking imperial and official on her yellow ear tag.

o

For some reason newspapers have been working their
way more and more into my day to day. Just this morning, I was reading about the resolution by Mayor Timothy
quoted in the *Enderbee Endtimes*:

> Whereas the current city limits include areas X, Y,
> Z, and whereas new Strategy Megaproject Advance-
> ment is planned for undetermined areas ZZ, YY, XX,
> whose developers wish to integrate into municipal
> utilities, be it resolved that municipal boundaries be
> extended to maximize the tax base from oil and gas
> and other industry. We have undertaken this resolu-
> tion by council because of the economic benefits for
> the community.

This was maybe less surprising than the prose poems
that have started showing up in the *TroutSource* arts portal:

> When the land is swept up in non-local forces it means
> a vendetta of the heart, an uprising in the blood against
> the takers of the shiny recollection. Livelihood of cherries
> on a withering tree. Cradle land. Connection so strong it
> persists like experiences of infancy in the aging voice. The
> radicals sprout from the site of erasure.

When it isn't the news sneaking into our lives, it's the
gossip. Some would say about me that he has no wife, has
no son, but that Innisfree has the look of land cared for

by a mother and looked after by son. And that comment would make me hoarse and I would stop the wagon and I'd get us doing some berry-picking and I would breathe loudly into the bushes. Sometimes visitors will help me out financially. Especially if I tell them the sob story of a poor sop like me.

o

On days when nothing's going right and the future seems wrong, nights when what you do is a pitchfork in the face of another and what others do breaks both your big toes, it's time for a good scream. Ain't that right, Artsy Boy?

Nothing fancy. Just need your knee-high, repurposed duck-hunting boots for navigating them murk pools. And forest rich enough to sponge the high sounds of the scream too.

First Dan-the-Man hops from the wagon, jaw muscles knit, with permanently flexed abdomen that's a washboard even though he sits on his butt most of the day doing computer stuff. He stands on a glowing green stump in the pregnant lostness of fog, warming up his lungs, big buddy that he is.

Even Mayor Timothy was at the scream gathering, he who is always a good sport for any activity popular with residents, because the quarter moon in springtime marks the Solstice of our Strange Mood, the accumulations of the bad stuff overflowing in the cleanse of these times. Which are the times when we go for a scream.

Hip to hip on our plank of a seat, just before twilight, I guide the wagon to the back of the property, the reins dangling from the shoulders of the elk which tend to be out of sight in the leafage as they pull the creaky wagon forward, though their necks strain and sway this way and that as they pause to eat leaves. To where the fields meet the rising alpine at Scylla Ridge, which is where the best forest is, where mist mixes with fog and clouds prevail, and the scent is of wet stones or dry stone depending.

Arsty Boy gets his video camera ready, adjusting the gloom settings, because he is in the habit of filming the scream. We must look frazzled through that lens, our rashes glowing burgandy in the moment.

We all take places along a hillside where the poplars and cottonwood are with coloured shoots. We start moving our feet, doing little circle shuffles. Dan-the-Man is taking a while to warm up, so it's really Memily who starts the good scream with her rising wail, and she straightens both arms and stretches them far as possible, locking her elbows and spreading her fingers just as wide as they will go, palms flat. The screams are what Artsy Boy calls feral, the ripped sheet metal of some tooth-grinding shared ache of the community, a chorus of shouting and squealing, because the screamers are flawed, the screamers are held back, the screamers are weighted wrong. The screams themselves soar high, they do, into the forest, released into the aboveness, take the form of a greater starry night howl, the most buried conflict, our most pent-up frustration. Howl, growl. Find your spot—a stump, a rock, a knoll—walk in patterns with no symmetry, raise your hands to your neck or place on hips, or cupped round mouth, and yell, yell, scream, shriek whatever sound is in the lungs. Scream into the brush, the sky, bring a trumpet and blow.

The animals are cool with that, says Artsy Boy.

And when you have yelled long enough, the elk come out from the shadows, and they bugle too.

Well, that happened once.

After the scream tour, we shuffle over to Memily's. Scoured by our screaming, the soul skin raw and ripe and ready to reform like velvet. Screaming makes me sense the world different. Foreheads moist and warm-coloured, shoulders hanging natural from the release.

Memily has got these dead logs erected vertically and also sections of old metal hydro poles with these sports balls suspended at the top of each of them from some invisible lines.

Over the past weeks we'd seen her making this stuff with Dan-the-Man in the distance, but knew it would be a surprise later revealed.

We eat stuffed zucchinis and get talking, and then Dan seems frustrated by something and departs, leaving us where we are under the tartan blankets draped around our thighs and waists, and it is me and Samson and Memily sitting around a flame garden that is copper-green and delphinium-blue, and I ask her about the I's that are set against the navy-hued, lower part of the sky.

She gets up and retrieves a jar of water and sits, twisting the metal lid off, having a sip that makes her lip look long through the glass. She swallows neat, twisting the lid back in place and setting the jar down by her feet by the cut log section she is sitting on.

Well, it's tough to explain, she says.

Let me say, let me just say I love it, says Samson. Great artwork, hiccup.

I am calling it a *field of i's*, says Memily. It's about . . . it's about how within even a person or the identity of a town there's more than one of them. Like the I that goes to work, and the I that goes to a party, those are different. And it is also my way of telling the forces that be that if you fuck with the land, you fuck with me.

Duhhh, okay, I like it, I like it I guueeesss, I say low, directing the tip of a long stick into the fire and scratching my white beard because of the tiredness that comes in the fields.

I love the art, says Samson, jumping up and doing a ninja elk farmer kick like I taught him.

They say there is another type of I, says Dan-the-Man, who has reappeared and is now speaking from behind one of the poles and also hidden by the mauve dogwood boughs. Sometimes he gets wistful and wanders off like that, and Memily will go searching for him with a torch and find him standing stock-still and silent somewhere in the night fields or by forest edges.

Another type of I? I say to both Dan and Memily. You don't say.

Yes, an I that's susceptible to the power of suggestion, Dan-the-Man says with an almost Gregorian voice, peering off into the nocturnal fields that are scattered with shining lines of wet plants.

Well, says Memily, for another thing, you never remember the actions of the action I, because those actions happen when your other I's off playing or sleeping or lying down like an underscore symbol.

Dan shuffles his sandals. Or like . . . like . . . the hornets were hovering in the heat, he says, putting the heal of his hand to the slab of his forehead.

Memily throws a little water at his toes from the jar,

and Dan snaps to attention.

Look, this is flake talk, he says suddenly. Like your other barn, Jeffery.

Err, okay, I say. I put a hand on Samson's shoulder to lead him away. As we move off through the bushes, over the shadowy grass that has not a stone to trip up a single toe, back to Innisfree, Dan heckles us again:

It's twisted hippie shit what you are up to over there, he says. Your sense of smell is shot, Inkster. It smells like death in that barn.

As I escort Artsy Boy away, I think: Sure as hell I may not understand the whole world, but I know who I am.

No worries, Samson, I say. Let's go this a-way. No worries. It was a good scream, let us go, let us go now. Memily, I suggest helping the gentleman to sleep, he obviously over-screamed or something.

o

Yes indeedy, the tours and other duties must go on despite the terror threats from the outside, and a place like
Innisfree Ranch has become a desired oasis. After the
spring scream the touring business picks up, and now
with the first tour group complete, all the visitors a tad
more four-legged than they were before, I had a mind to
take out my gurdy and play a number and tell the good
old ElkBoatHumans foundational tale, when I heard the
black truck coming, and that triggered something that
tensed up my back muscles, and I fell to my knees, shaking in the shoulders and thighs. A father and son came
over and asked me what was wrong and I told them one
of the trucks with fittings clanging down the road, as the
hard rubber wheels jounced over the washboard, that's
what was wrong, and it was battering my nerves. One of
the trucks that stinks something terrible and rattles along
and never stops in public places because of the fumes
that leak out of the valves when it's still. The same type
that fishtailed off the road over there in the dead area of
the ranch. Feels as though the fluid that spilled out of the
flipped truck is contaminating the corner of my acreage
once again, twenty years later.

Dangerous goods always going back and forth on roads
the colour of dried blood, through the fields and forests
of the shared treaty lands. Sometimes I say to my neighbours as we walk along through the town: Be careful of
the dangerous good. It is the good that comes from an
obsession.

The future is scattered in little pieces around the present. It gets better. No, it gets worse. When the whole world is like a slapped thing, tingling with coming bruise, it gets worse.

I, I, I.

I yank a squealing Hyperion IV by his ear tag to the Other barn. I lead him over to the pillory and get his head in the hole, then hobble his legs. Then bring the pillory bar down and fasten the iron hasps onto the elk torso.

o

The antlers are seventeen weeks' mature, pulsing in their soft, blood-filled, pre-calcified state. I put the bar of the saw to the base of the mauve horn and press the trigger, begin to slice the glowing antler off. My earplugs muffle the sound of the Hyperion's scream.

Something in the air making everyone dizzy, to be certain, and maybe a little bit daft and confused too. From all the new industry sweeping westward. This is the third wave, this is the fourth or fifth generation of the drillsbury doughboy doing his thing in these parts. The area from here to the coast used to feel just trampled. Now it's stomped flat like land dough. And the dizziness of big projects is more from stomach illness, though it started as love. Like some sort of hypnosis, where everything is pleasant and carefree. But something foul-tasting is marinated in the bliss, so that something disgusting is made to sound like it would be tasty.

There used to be many around here doing good, even great stuff. When I say that people left, which is something I say, I mean a percentage of the people.

Those who stayed on were those who could keep the dream stoked, who excelled at the smalling of the bigger things. But the early radical folks were pushed more into the hills. Some of them took on monitoring roles. Innisfree always existed on the other side of the disputes, where everyone and everything got along just fine together.

After sawing one of the antlers off, then the other, put the two into a metal bucket, then bring them over to the processing unit, and release them into the grinder hole, which crushes them into a blood pulp.

o

After the velvet is sealed and off to southern processing facilities, we go to the li'l town of Byzantium, to the stone bank to deposit the elk profit to the elk coffers. We pass the fawn shop and there is an elk mount on the wall above a stereo—the fusion of ferocity and finesse that is Wapiti.

Artsy Boy exclaims, Elk!

I reply that it isn't any elk. Just a mount, a mock-up of life.

But its hollowed corpse, Mr. Inkster, looks fierce and bold. Looking alive means something, doesn't it? To which I say yes, part of the soul is in the fur and skin and nails and teeth, but the rest is gone to somewhere . . . down below.

Little is known about skeletal growth in elk, said Stu Keck's elk website.

And on the Innisfree website, it says:

HARDEN YOUR CARTILAGE
GIVE YOUR MUSCLES AND BRAIN MORE TORQUE
TURBOCHARGE YOUR IMMUNE SYSTEM
ERADICATE PAIN TO GET A STRUT ON YOUR DREAMS
FEEL FRESH AS WILD TIGER LILY NECTAR
BECOME THE BEDROOM BEAST WITH THE LEAST
FLACCIDITY
WITH OL' JEFFERY INKSTER'S VELVET ANTLER POWDER
THE ANCIENT ORIENTAL TRADITION IN
THE CAN'TADIAN NORTHWEST

What might feel to you like just a minor discomfort or a normal lack of energy, will, if left unremedied, escalate to more serious problems involving pain and torpor later in life. Taking elk powder elixir each week is proven to resolve slow-growing joint issues, and solve the long-term lack of gallop in one's life.

Bombing No Laughing Matter?

25 June 2037—*Troutsource Art*

In art news related to the bombings, an international satellite in Free Space has managed to perform a language MRI of the pipeline plot, though the location remains scrambled due to Enderbee's hazy coordinates. The iterated text translation of the bomber's actions came out as what seems to be prose poetry in the satellite decoder.

Gravy To Overthrow the Cheese Curds, a radical humour cyber NGO, has posted the poetic interpretations of the industrial sabotage on their decipherment page. *Pipe Watch*, an industry security watchdog that employs ten thousand pipe observers, recently hired a team of Harvard- and Sorbonne-educated poetry scholars to decode the prose poem progression that the satellite scan is picking up.

"The sequential nature of the poem," said *Pipe Watch* think tank director Derrida Bloom, "makes the form recall a pipeline itself, with a plot that goes through in a gush of symbolism."

It is *Pipe Watch's* hope that this "prose poem progression," once interpreted, will mean something, namely the revelation of the bombers' identity and location. Though Derrida Bloom remains mystified about any stable interpretation so far.

The anti-hero, as we can tell by the first prose poem in the progression, is attempting to lie still as s/he waits for the moment to strike.

Follow this visualized interpretation of the prose poem on the *Podview* feature on the *Troutsource* website—your source for undiluted reality, the wilderness of perception, wellspring of revivified senses.

Sun still sets in Enderbee not orbital thought. Red navigation beacons across on Scylla Ridge to south. Charge in hand click tiny green light. Heptanitrocubane initialize signaller. Retreat back counting GPS metres away through the animal paths through the plant paths through the reptilian to the ancient mind to emerge. Now beating deep heart, press button, key to ignite button to blast what is forward. A moment of hesitation. AD 2026, AD 2027, AD 2028 . . . 2037 BCE. Bird noise. Bird peeps. Left margin to right margin. Calm. Future. Prison. Manacles. Ignition must wait. Retreat. Patrol copter coming. Return on down the stem of the Iron God's flute. The Bronze Tree's roots. Boreal camouflage. Charybdis ridge to north above quaint sleepy Byzantium along wall of survivor lilacs three kilometres up ridge. Smile of ancient monks of China grimace of sour Christian elect. Worldly inklings fragrant path into ferment of berries gorse and gargantuan leaves of cow parsnip. Know the animal paths back-of-hand known. Hunchwalk over mesa. Moment not precise, off by a nano-fraction. No past. No future. Story and fact collated. Twilight between worlds. Pegasus meets Moose. Toward the pipe, the pipe by the north peak of Charybdis Ridge. Blue spruce forest Engelmann eccentric. Above town drenched in prophetic oily shadow. Toward the pipe. Destroy what is forward.

o

What if PC Columbia and Cowberta had never redrawn their borders in the 2020s, if them there protesters had managed to stop the Enbridge Northern Gateway pipeline from going through? And the Can'tadian government upheld the moratorium on tankers along the northwest coast. Well, then the new Gasbro high pressure bitumen-lite line would never have reached the table today. On the other hand, Enderbee county would be but a speck of dust in our imaginations.

The history of Enderbee as Commons can actually be traced back to when one of the surveyors, who died by fungus-gas exposure at a morel processing plant not long ago, poor fella, forgot to correct his GPS numbers when he was working on borderland reform during the foundational years of Enderbee in the previous century. You see, the military throws in a variable of something like seven metres into the satellite grid at all times and, in order to correct the readings to get the adjusted coordinates, you have to wait a week until the military releases them online, at least that was the case back then.

Well, the surveyor forgot to correct his points, that angelic dumb-ass, and so an area just under 500 hundred square kilometres on the west side of the Rockies-Always-the-Rockies lacked definition within a necessary legal framework. That particular land title survey was as a consequence tossed out, and the old land sectioning map was applied. But the surveyors had screwed up back in the day too. On their maps were several missed areas, gaps between Dominion Land Survey grids, which fell outside the metes and bounds. Imagine one set of flawed blueprints pressed against another; it was that confusing for everyone involved. The land was declared Commons, because it was not in Can'tadian nature to fight over a meagre section, which also solved several other associated land claims, allowing a whole bunch of different folks to sign the most strange and new wave treaty of self-governance ever negotiated. That's Enderbee, one of those areas which is technically under the jurisdiction of both provinces, but is owned and overseen by the original First Nations and Allies as a heritage experiment. Daft Society Dodgers and other back-to-the-landers started moving to Enderbee. The mix-up became the happy truth for many, though local antlers are still locked over some discrepancies. Like sometimes they try to tell me that, according to PC agricultural law, I am not permitted to farm a native species like Wapiti, but I respond that I'll fight their stop-work order in court. Fact is, my case is a strong one, the Olympic elk isn't native to Enderbee; it's a coastal species. And if that argument isn't good enough, well, I can argue that I should be beholden to Cowbertan law, if any, in which case it would be a moot point, because you can breed animals like this there. In other words, we get away with stuff here in Enderbee.

○

I got in the habit of filling out identification cards with all the names of the folks around here, because I wanted to learn who out of all of the community could be so violent as to plan an atrocity that would make all of the treaty bonds insolvent. I kept the cards, and Artsy Boy helped me write most of them.

And this tracking of others had nothing to do with the reward money for finding the bomber, I might add.

The Carlyle family

SUMMARY: Won a two-million-dollar lottery in the '20s, but blew it all on expensive booze and retrofitting doodads for their eighty-some collector vehicles. Own and operate what some call a "greasy" refurbishing business somewhere in the full section boonies.

DESCRIPTION: Snotty children, velour riding pants, toothbrush stashes.

ALIASES: "The Car Family," "Thaaat House"

Samson said he'd been reading up on the current state of technology, and a project that aims to switch all the world's satellite images into kinds of poems, and that they are using poems to follow folks who are rubbing the world's back the wrong way, because, miraculously enough, the hidden information from these wrongdoers shows up in the poems even though it is invisible on the television or computer.

And that, my good friend Artsy Boy, was too much for me to follow. Though, it did sound like a perverse truth you might find in one of the books he's been lending out, like the one that slips between what he calls genres . . . Or was it genders and gendarmes? Or like the one that said on the back something along the lines of, "This novel reads like Richard Brautigan on brown acid."

Artsy Boy, not only the egg farmer, but also the wearer of the diarist's hat and the filmmaker's hat, he even went so far as to say that the elk too is in fact a prose poem. He learned me stuff like that about poetry. About how apparently it was an old parted haired chap named T.S. Eliot who denied the prose poem its status as poem, because poetry for him implied rules, and the prose poem had no rules because it had no line breaks to measure rules with. The prose poem always slips between slop buckets.

I had to agree with my ranch hand: elk are prose poems because they were never properly named, and there was always some confusion over exactly what they were, but that is guesswork.

●

Right margin to left margin. Left margin to right margin right margin to left margin. Pipeline full of ichor. Lights shine up on Charybdis, Byzantium down below. Scylla on other side. Enderbee top of funnel into eskers bordering myth. Camouflage has become utter invisibility. Encrypted remote. Clear. Sunday. Reconnect detonation device. Insert plastic mold into bore hole. Ammonium nitrate. Rocks along Scylla connect like chains. Trees are fence posts 'round, sheltering, treewell bunker, rotting trapper's cabin.

o

Sometimes me and the ranch hands will hike deeper into
the valleys beyond the valleys where the headwaters of
Lethe bubble and froth and spit forth from the mantle.
We canoe together there on a rare hot summer night. The
most recent time Artsy Boy wanted to take footage, so we
got our first recording of what it actually looks like. Cliffs
are high along the sides of Lethe where it gets to the Klap-
panadoix headwater area. When the moon comes out, we
dock on slabs of rock on the wall of the river and we eat
some meat of elk, and we drink wine of dandelion. By the
light of beetle-wood fires we paint on the walls of Lethe
in the images which were first found here. We paint all
night long: BoatElks and BoatHumans and ElkHumans
and ElkBoatHumans, all in a wild form, which I guess
makes sense for an all-night wall painting festival. And
so we do what the elk want in return for the life of their
antlers.

We fill elk-skin bladders in a tributary of Lethe called
Microchip. These waters help us remember times from
before. Yes, sometimes the drinking makes us experience
drelkams in which stuff from a supposed past appears,
like the Greek gods coming as fleas in the cuffs of the
early land agents, and on boats where they stowed in European books damp from the paddle's spray. We remember how titans transformed into animals, and how they
are threatened again by the Olympians of industry. We
remember, but we forget. We remember that Zeus was a

resource developer and that Mnemosynes and Hyperions threatened that regime with the tradition they still have saddled on their backs from the times before the Olympians were in power. And we forget. How tangled are the myths that inform this place.

o

After our most recent sip from the Microchip tributary, around the time the pipeline bombings started, a memory became clear to me of the early twenty-first century when the first professional hypnotist came to Byzantium. I remember his loose sweater, his thin wrists shrunken like they'd been butch once. Like an Olympian getting over a sickness or something, was the man with the strange name I cannot quite place. Had the skills to get the audience to make action out of their emotion. People with interesting skills like the hypnotist's are always coming to town, but they often don't stay long because they think rural life doesn't offer enough expanding room. Some leave a real impression on a town, though, and I will always remember that hypnotist's shows, how he held sway over all the people in the barroom, how he made . . . us . . . do and say those things. His name, it started with an M . . . One of his hypnotic techniques was having us repeat the words *left margin to right margin right margin to left margin*, over and over again. Now that line always comes back to me, as I think it does to others who went to the show. In the same way that a popular song leaves a permanent mark on your mind.

But life is full of important realizations that in the moment seem life-altering, and even those world-exploding lessons are soon forgot.

Go get another elk, lead it into the Other barn. Repeat procedure. With all 440, that's about 900 velvet antlers. Grind them up, dry the pulp, and then ship to Cancougar to get processed into packaged powder supplements and tested by the CFDA.

o

When you hear the fingers snap, the performer had said. *"Snap out of it."*

The performer dressed in grey janitor gear with key ring on hip that chimed in the night. He used a metal staff like a third leg to move around the barroom. I was still conscious, knew it was towards another participant he was directing his powers. But to whom?

When you hear the snap, the person you love most in the room, who you find most attractive—go up and let them know. You. Are. In. Love. With. Them.

First snap, and the participant's neck went limp and his hat slumped forward on his head somehow without falling off. After a pause that contained the sound of the light bulb whining and the ringing of quiet bells, the second snap came, and the participant's shoulders seemed to straighten alert, and he lifted his head again, though with eyes still slit. He rose limply to his feet, then floated up to someone seated at one of the tables. Was it Memily he approached and serenaded? In my memory it was Memily. Then that participant, tan-hat guy, must have been Dan-the-Man? I can't see into the back of the barroom because of the vapour clouds and gloom lighting, but I can hear the volunteer's proposal to the person back there, to Memily, must be. Whoever to whoever: *I love you like the waterfall does the fall.* That's what was said back there, love words of all sorts, and that's where the "lovin' all da time" song got inspired, it occurs to me now.

Then the hypnotist turned another key in the hovering

54

air, telling a second volunteer to go out the back door of the pub and pluck a blade of grass. When the subject did this, leaving dreamily and returning with a blade that fit well between her thumbs, the hypnotist asked her what she had learned from it. *I am going to play in a blade of grass band, said the volunteer. The real blue joint grass.*

The third volunteer had to light a cherry bomb in a jar out back as well.

And then, what happened next?

Then the singing of the bird in the shadows. The Elk-head above the hearth, shifting.

o

I was tossing alfalfa pellets into the eating troughs, then had moved on to the antlers—my last task to perform by daylight. When I was heading into the farmhouse for the night, wiping bits of blood off my hands with a rag, a beetle-black station wagon had crept up the shale driveway, parked by the welcome sign that says "Greekings, Elksters!" A person who looked like he wasn't from here, not from anywhere near close to here because of his fancy overcoat, clopped briskly through the fog in a direct line towards the farmhouse porch.

Hello.

Oh, hello Mars.

Shook his hand. Gloves were golden leather, wranglers. The grip frail, yet tight.

What was that noise coming from back there, Mr. Inkster? Sounds like someone's molesting a duck.

He pointed back into the hut where I'd just come from. Frost blew from our nostrils and the whorls appeared to shake hands between us.

Just the elk making the noises they do, I said.

He gave me a shadowed stare from under the rim of a hat that looked more like an ancient helmet, pleated zinc, because of a synthetic kind of lustre. He stomped the shank of his boots on each stair, exposing socks that had trident prints on them.

Listen, I'm a straight-up guy. Here to ask some questions about the bombings. I've been doing the rounds of Byzantium and the greater area of Enderbee, collecting stories. That's what I do: I find the real story out of the fakes. I'm also here to collect my dues.

Nothing but real stories here on Innisfree, and in the wider county of Enderbee, I said.

Offered him some coffee. He was suddenly not the tough guy anymore. His talk became soothing. He reminded me of a sleepy bird. Nice as a lazy afternoon on a garden patio. Nice as butter, nice as pie, nice as a cream soda spritzer. The more he spoke, the more he became familiar from a long time ago, but changed somehow too.

How long have you owned the ranch? he asked—

Twenty years, I replied.

And that's why you keep turning down our offers?

Yes.

Easy, easy answers, I think to myself. Questions so simple their repetition makes me doze.

Fair enough, Jeffery. Now, I am going to give you these two bags, old-fashioned duffle bags, and I want you to put them somewhere you just won't remember. Okay?

Yes, Mars Ares.

Now, good, that's under the floorboards. Now, here (he snapped his fingers a couple times and repeated something under his breath). You have prepared the elk powder for us?

Yes, lots of elk powder for you, Mars.

Good boy. Now give me all the powder.

Yes, Mars Ares.

And make sure to saw their antlers soon as they're pushed, 'kay.

Yes, Mars Ar—but . . . Wait a sec now, who the?

He showed me a picture of an elk chewing on flowers.
Forget. Forget. That's it. Forget.

○

The sounds of the Swainson thrush in the evening is the most musical birdsong you could imagine. Thrilling is the music before nightfall coming in through the windows of the farmhouse. The winds out of the skyahhh, with the birdsong from twilight's design in the trees. Some folks around here, when I say "skyahhh," they say, "*Huh*. What?" They say, "You said something . . . Did you say Gaia? What does that mean, Mr. Inkster?" I shake my head. I say things funny from being with the elk for so long. What I really said was "in the sky," with an accent following it. Sometimes I use a long a, or it sounds like I do, on the end. My mom's side were from Constantinople. Accentuate funny. I don't know what they mean by Gaia. I said skyahhh!

o

Yuppers, Artsy Boy Samson saw something when playing back the images of Lethe, which is the river that cuts along the northwest corner of the property. What he saw he thought should not have shown up on film because it was of another non-sensory spectrum or sump'n. Real hazy footage. Of some sort of sabotage carried out by bodies difficult to know, unidentifiable because the old tape is partly decomposed and the image sludge-lined. But me, I am not so far gone in the rustic world that I can't see a screen and tell what's going on through the distortion. They're battering cement in a pickle bucket, pasting a main valve at a metering station with cement laced with shotgun shells.

Samson reported having sipped from the Microchip tributary in order to remember, and realized that we are, as servants of elk, also gatekeepers to the Elkhead, and that I should be warned—spirit-bodied thieves will try using tactics to confuse and besmirch us to get at the knowledge of Innisfree. What he says is in line with what I feel has been happening: that something has put paid to the dream of Innisfree. When I asked Samson who he's making these videos for, though, he got mealy-mouthed. And I had to tell him, if it's for someone you don't know below the surface of appearance, and who you forget after you see them, then don't give them the video clips, because they are using that to get at the Elkhead. Then Samson became the one calling me paranoid. Paranoia has no place on Innisfree, I agree with him. But what used to be called paranoia is now a more than partial truth, like Border Patrol taking DNA samples from townsfolk and rural groups who live near the pipelines, which is going way too far for Enderbee. Sampling the copper in our veins, I guess you could say, but without drilling rights. Taking hair clippings and little pieces of skin from our cuticles. Over-obvious investigators, using their over-obviousness to make us uneasy, since the reward system hasn't worked for bringing the crickets outta the cracks. So their game of niceties is at an end.

I am involved in the bombing only in that I support the bomber's cause, I told them—as in industry should steer clear from the real preciousness out here—but I am not the bomber. Trust is what this place is built on, I might add, foundations stronger than money, and now you are trying to break apart the bonds that hold the trust, through trying to plot the poetry of the town and country, which is how bad things happen with counties and countries and all the land under the sun.

Samson just said: C'mon, Inkster, what you say we wet your noodle with some corncob bombs.

Uhm, Samson? Pass me a card.

o

Loads of suspicious people in these parts. Even someone you trust.

Samson Huckleberry

SUMMARY: Organic egg farmer and artistic ranch hand. Keeps all his chickens in a "hen palace." A bit crazy.

DESCRIPTION: Looks like The Littlest Hobo who never grew up.

ALIASES: "Artsy Boy," "The Eggstatic Juggler"

o

Why me, why here, why this? Well, as a child in the 1980s the notion of the elk life first formed when I saw the specialists firing nets from a herding helicopter. These zoologists were busy leashing Olympic elks on hillsides to better study how much of each shrub they chomp per square foot of brush. Helping with those Ministry studies was how I learned to get the wild behind a fence, which makes a man proud and gives a soul a sense of control.

Enderbee County, being near the foot plains of the Rockies-Always-the-Rockies, was a good—the best—choice for the farm, with its streams for habitat and irrigation, its uncommon wetness and heat.

We did slaughter the elk for a time during the Flesh-wasting Disease scare, when the trade borders snapped shut because of infection, and we still sacrifice one percent of the herd annually for the tour meals. Oh, and then there was the safari hunts, but I didn't get along so well with the clients.

Ceased naming my elk Mnemosyne and Hyperion during times we were slaughterers for the flesh-wasting cull, and during the safari. Only so much of this slaughter a person can take before they start to feel like the bad guy in a hacker movie, which is not something we like to think about too deeply on Innisfree. Still, I sometimes catch myself assessing the meatiness of one of my ranch hand's ribs, like Artsy Boy's, but he's a slim one. Just kidding.

o

The June tours are tough because they happen during the velvet harvest, so we are busy at the Other barn, and there are questions that need to be avoided and places on the property that have to be steered clear from, especially when the animal inspectors come. If it isn't the sensitiveness of the folks to the process, then it's the prudery of the city classes in face of the elks getting physical, sometimes in what tourists find an inappropriate manner. I might chide a group of college students about the one-antlered elk so lonesome. Look how he licks the air, wishing it were the tenderness of a maharaja. That Hyperion fought other stags for this chance at love and now he is hopelessly hungry. That's the ache that drives mammals crazy. The ache from loneliness is one thing, but the hurt from physical longing is a tremor of want. I tell them about the female orgasm and how the anus is a beautiful part of the body and how there is stuff in manure that smells good. Sometimes the tour groups don't come back to Innisfree, but sometimes they laugh, they do, and sometimes they realize that holding a tongue is like pinching a vein, really not healthy. Look at the elk. Yes, they mate. Yes, they roll in urine as a kind of perfume. I told the people on the tour this stuff as I steered the wagon around the back spurs of the hills.

o

Mine elk are in fact Olympic elk, I boast to the group. Of the Wapiti overarching variety. The biggest non-extinct kind, yes sir. And you know the name of the elk has a ghost history. They were called stags by European settlers who thought what they were seeing was the red deer like back home. But they always thought, gosh, this sure is a big stag I killed. The English in particular called elk "elk," but they were using the word in reference to the European moose, which they thought they saw lumbering over their homesteads here, called "elk" overseas, but which is actually quite different than the North American moose. Settlers also learned the Algonquin Indian term "moose," but that didn't stick well when applied to the strange stags that we now know as the Wapiti elk, because of the obvious differences between the lumbering moose and its straight-shouldered relative. Eventually they did learn the word Wapiti, but to this day some dictionaries define it wrong, saying it means deer. Elks were not so easy to name to the explorers, but the First Nations' name stuck like they usually do, along with the Greek names.

The Wapiti was a beast that said no to our attempts to categorize it. Which is why they are truly mythical to me. I don't slaughter the elk anymore, unless they get lame or get the disease. I do do the tourist thing, sure, and I do do the other thing, which some people don't like.

o

Hey Inkster, wondering if you would mind coming over 'ere (Artsy Boy has what he calls his "Super 8" pointed at me again. He's wearing clam diggers and old-style loafers). Come on, I'm going to film you by the alfalfa.

Wants to film me throwing some feed into the troughs, the thing being the magnificent sky giving the look he wants. Falling alfalfa through the rays like it was the Euphrates and this was a sun initiation.

Cry some real Hollywood tears in front of that *Gone With the Wind* sunset, says he.

Samson has a way of twisting my arm, bringing out the media clown in me. Find myself speaking all sorts of words when he films. Words that really aren't like me. Like I'm playing the part of an elk farmer. This Artsy Boy sure has managed to stir things up at Innisfree, coming from the media soak of the Big Smoke, as he did. He's a hard-working young man, but he gets cheeky and over-confident sometimes. The threat statements from the bombers are really rousing him.

You're holding strong against those Gasbro bastards. You have for years. You are the leader, the fearless leader of Innisfree, if not of all Enderbee. Now, hold up the alfalfa, Inkster. And tell us what it's all about.

Well, if you haveta know, this here is alfalfa, an Arab-named crop which we grow on Innisfree. Means king. The king of plants. There. Now we haveta go put some more fence up where the rutting Hyperion have torn it apart. And get the salt licks. And warsh the walls of the

Other barn. Turn off that infernal gun camera. This is no time for gurdy and games.

Hold it up. Hold it up to the sun. One more time.

Mnemosyne XXVI and Hyperion IV follow my hand cupping the alfalfa wistfully, their snouts jumping about, as I ham it for the camera again.

An elk projection for others to see? Come, my tourists, come to the elk farm and ride the carriage through the hills of Innisfree. Elk will drag all your worries away and make you happy like me. Give me a break . . .

Ranch hands go single file out of the walk-in freezer, arms stacked high with freshly cut velvet antlers, to the cooling truck for shipment.

The population of Enderbee is booming, according to a report from the federal housing agency.

o

Samson has taken it upon himself to film the many tributaries of Lethe and share what a bitumenlite rupture would threaten, and his enthusiasm for a renewed program of elk worship made us all happier in the face of the resource war going on in the woods and fields around Innisfree. When he visited neighbour Memily to wish her a happy thirty-ninth birthday as I told him he should, he fell promptly into colour with her, and they talked about art all night. Maybe Dan-the-Man's nose snuffled underneath the upstairs sheets in jealousy, but probably not, because jealousy hardly exists in a beautiful, alternative place like this. Artsy Boy now pens a letter to Memily inspired by their conversation.

Memily, I have fallen into colour with you, just like Inkster predicted I would. As the years pass through Innisfree, I almost feel like I am becoming an oldster who needs to keep communicating his thoughts, otherwise they might disappear. We are editing our Lethe footage now. I just adore images. And sounds. And words. Especially of Lethe: where the river braids, and the light strikes, there are currents of black, currents of chrome, currents of pewter and of coal—braids of dark tintage. It's like the substance of mythological dreams at our fingertips. Amazing how the patterns work, coming through the dark springs in the ground from the Klappanoix. It becomes more full of nutrients the farther the water gets from the underwater chambers, and it's strange to see the blooms of blue algae along the banks of clear water. We are guiding the film, but the process is some-

how beyond us. It works its way through the images. As we go through the footage we try to feel out where those patterns might occur. We are showing how forms decompose when the wide angle is broken into thousands of tiny points of view. How unexpected forms arise, bob up out of those rhythms. There are many talented artists and scientists seeing through, objectively, to those rhythms. I am really glad to have met you, Memily. You have a penetrating sense, I'd even say that you somehow feel, or feelingly conceive, very deeply, and it comes across in how you do your art, with such colour that one falls into . . . Could this be love? I don't want to piss off Dan-the-Man. What you have between you must last. The life that you and others in Enderbee fashion from the territory is inspiring, and really, it's going to be the only way . . . gardening, canning, reusing, helping, seeing, collaborating, and being sufficient unto ourselves, to live, as the superstructure comes a-tumbling down. Crazy for some to have thought this century would be the end of history. It's merely the beginning.

o

Enderbee council was the only city council I know of to have a cross-dresser member, but then they were not re-elected and now Cheryl Hill lives down the pipe from me, even deeper into the mountains. The first time I spoke to Cheryl, zhe told me zhe hated labels and that to speak words was to fall into a world of compartments and that I could say anything but never should I call zher a tranny or transvestite, because it made it sound like how a scientist might name a spider.

During zher brief time as city councillor back in the early 20s, zhe had a great ear for the concerns of ordinary people like me. Zhe was somebody who seemed to have an ability to make the sides disappear in a city hall debate and make every point of view relevant.

To this day, my distant neighbour, clothed in some contrariwise dress, is firebrand when the town needs to wag a finger at some hag.

Remember what Cheryl said: I don't like men who wave their pipes around, not one bit. Cold. Cold. Put that pipe back in your pants, you bitumen fiend!

It was back then with the heated debates at city hall between Councillor Hill and Mayor Timothy that perhaps the first seeds of what would come were sewn amongst the townsfolk. Soon the torches came out, so to speak, and it was hard times for Cheryl Hill and in fact for most of us on the treaty lands.

Cheryl Hill

SUMMARY: Crossover and recently drama performer. Lives by the lake zhe calls Naked Walden.

DESCRIPTION: Zhe has dogs and geese and goes out on the highway and walks kilometres and kilometres dressed in pink ballerina drag.

ALIASES: "Cottage Puffin," "Thoreau's Fantasy"

o

Then Byzantium city hall got a new municipal crest in the front, and Artsy Boy was commissioned to create it. I was admiring his work as I waited for the meeting.

The new crest of a golden drill rig. The old crest was two people hand-sawing a tree next to a hoe suspended in the air.

I was looking at this and thinking about transformations and contradictions when I heard rusted engines clattering about. Turning from the crest, I saw one of the Carlyle kids sauntering over the manicured grass with a coyote-like lope.

Member of a dynasty of small farmers in the same general area as Innisfree Ranch. Farmers who have been there a heck of a lot longer than the likes of me and who weren't signed onto the treaty, and who don't agree with much or care for anyone except themselves, pretty much.

Turns out the Carlyle boy, he's petitioning local government on behalf of his father who is probably drunk on an outdoor sofa in the field right about now. The family wants the derby grounds protected and not to have to move because of the fracking rigs.

The Carlyle boy looks fifteen, even though he must be twenty-something by now. The kid who years back used to chuck burrs at the elks, leaning over the wagon like he's leaning now on the brick municipal building wall with his own collar curling round his neck like tin-fitting. Cow tipping . . . fine . . . but elk tipping? I don't think so, little Carlyle. That was going too far.

Me, I'm dressed in my old city duds. You know: the leather patches and the metal stamps in the pocket tops and my good striped shirt completely unfaded.

Turns out the Carlyle boy was at the city council meeting like me to make a fuss to city representatives.

I was there to see a presentation by Cheryl Hill on transgender rights and also to demand to know more about the city's land agent permitting policy—there's a mouthful for ya—to tell council they should make agents register as companies, or at least, keep track of them. Because of the weird land agents who have been a-coming on my land and how the city can't tell me nothing about them. That's right, nothing at all, I said. And brought my hand down on the podium to accentuate the point I was trying to make.

Council on that day was passing a resolution to the union of municipalities to have more say over what happens beyond city limits, and it meant dealing with those in the treaty lands like us on Innisfree, even though out there we don't have an official town hall, nothing like that.

The councillors seemed to all have these wobbly smiles and these daydreamy stares. And around them on the walls of the council chamber was a new fresco that showed a valley seen from the sky, and it looked pristine, untouched like. I think Artsy Boy helped with that one too.

When the Carlyle boy made his presentation, he remarked about the waste of money the fresco was.

But when I presented, I told council, Hey, damned if I

can't see Innisfree somewhere in that fresco behind yous.

Mayor Timothy was bemused and distant. And deeply satisfied.

o

Outside on the street after the meeting, I told the Carlyle boy he needed to learn where to place the silver spoon at these meetings with business and local officials, and that way he'd get farther in his search for justice. Don't insult their artwork, in other words, was my wisdom. There's an order to the dining room table that mother teaches you.

You know what? he shot back. I'd take that spoon and I'd spit right on it. Or stick it in a cow pie I'd slap on the table next to their glazed duck and chestnuts. If I dined with royalty.

The Carlyle boy swung open the door of his old Chevy and flopped sideways onto the bench seat, shoving his doobie into the overflowing ashtray and grinding the manual shift stick.

He's right, I thought. A change is happening in the order of the leading heads that sit around the tables in the long houses of the mountains. That he has right.

o

A coyote carcass was found on a tour that week, it was, and it was flat, just bones and pelt.

It's a coyote pancake, I said to the father and son who made the discovery.

Breakfast for lunch? said the father, joking, to the disgust of the son.

If you want a colon full of worms, I said.

There are some realities of elk life that don't sit well, I continued. Such as the fact that they'll trample ya flat if you get too close to them. They'll squeeze out your guts like lemongrass from a tube.

Another reality of elk life is the fact that the farm does get disease sometimes for which cures must be found. Like a while back, someone asked what the redness on my arms was, but I couldn't go so far as to tell them that, even if I knew the cause and name of the condition. We get it sometimes. We get rid of the elks who have it right quick. But I got it. And I need the pipe carrier to help get healed, because there's no medication can cure this rash. And come to think of it, another problem could be one of reputation, you see, and the things people think of when they don't know about the velvet process. Like someone at the Enderbee Smokery will tell a visitor, "Hey, why not visit Inkster's hobby farm and see if he's selling some ceremonial meats." With the emphasis here being on the word hobby. They would say, "Stay away from the 'Other' Barn," with the emphasis on Other.

Of course the shops that cater to the visitors don't have any problem selling the products of the Other barn.

A visitor will notice the willow and poplar trees, how they appear rotten 'round the trunks. "Ah, what happened to your trees?" they will say. I tell them: The elk bite all the bark off, and they rub up against the trunks in the fall rut. They can rub the life out of a small forest.

Like a person who can slit the throat of a tree by the girdling method, where they cut a strip of bark off with two metal scythes. That's the same thing that the elk do to trees, using their backs to grind down the skin.

o

The general reality of things is that they have become very "correct." Too correct, if you please. Sometimes foreign visitors ask what the PC means in PC Columbia. I thought it was a widely known fact, but I guess not, so maybe I should say it stands for Politically Correct.

Hey, I said to one of the people on the tour. Look at that, the elk are having sex.

I'd prefer if you said mating, said the man. Don't like to say the word sex in front of my son. Especially in this nature context.

You're probably one of those who says "passed away" instead of "dies?" I replied.

Well, come to think of it, said the man, you may be correct about that.

You have to be frank about stuff, I said.

Can we see the velvet antler process, the man asked.

Uhm. No.

Did I mention the Cow in Cowberta stands for Cash Cow, because that's where the money was and also the oil is and was, and it's there that the money is going. The oil life wasn't the way of life in the Northwest Coast until the Cow came trampling through.

o

I was tight-fisted about arguing for surface rights, just like all of us in Enderbee were, except for maybe the Carlyles, what with their shield-engraved loyalty to progress—though don't mess with the Carlyles if the derby grounds are affected. Me, damn right I refused when Gasbro said it wanted to put a well on my property according to the mineral rights. Would you let a stranger put a furnace in the middle of your living room? But progress did what progress would, a craving arm that can reach around a period of sobriety and regain its grip. So the plans of progress find their way around my ranch, one pipe, two pipe, and now some proposed high-pressure thing. I put up enough of a fuss that they didn't drill on my property, but they sure have done other stuff that may as well be right on my property. Innisfree had transformed into an island amidst squid-laced pipes and wildcat wells. I complained to city council about the Gasbro bloody bastard proposal, just like everybody else did. But folks from the Anti-Eco-Terrorist Squad are poking around these days. Even in the woods this feeling of maybe cameras hidden in pine cones.

Some people around here, like Samson, have been told by the doctors that they suffer from paranoia, and now he has to take little brain eggs that the weird roosters lay. City sickness has infected Enderbee. I can sense the uptightness welling up in my own raised fists, which I don't like, don't like at all.

It all got weird, real weird, after I told people at the city that a person named Mars Ares, nice as butter but strange as grasshopper, had been coming around to investigate the farms and entering our houses like a companionable but not entirely trustworthy stranger. The oil and gas commission, the police, could tell me nothing about this supposed land agent, or his operation. Mars Ares didn't exist, according to their records. It took me some time to make the connections that needed to be made. I knew the name, but where I knew it from, and the places I may have encountered that figure, were voids.

Locals Challenge Multinational

—19 September 2037—

A group of farmers have issued a court challenge against regional fossil fuel giant Gasbro.

The group, led by a coalition including ex-Byzantium council member Cheryl Hill and local artist and art teacher Memily Assange, takes aim at what they say are misleading health claims of land agents, in light of disturbing findings from a grassroots air-monitoring program.

A Buddhist retreat at the Northwest Doga cancelled all its sittings and eventually shut down permanently in face of the noise disturbances of helicopter and bulldozers working near the meditation quarters, and is part of the class action lawsuit along with whale conservationists and the farmers' coalition.

"Rita Ohm was told by the land agent that the right-of-way being designed by the linear proponent would not interfere with the chaotic garden of the retreat land," the coalition said in a public statement.

"The definition of pristine has been called into question by the companies to justify their agenda," the statement continues. "Remains of an old CN Rail grade through the area prove, according to the proponent, that the activist's PR depictions of an untouched wilderness are misleading."

o

When the landsman came, he was just so darn nice, and was actually there just to paint a pleasant landscape using watercolours very much in the style of a young painter in Vienna prior to the Second World War. Setting up an easel on the hillside.

The man with the name that another reckoned was from the old schools of Europe, he had a platform and a purpose that was tough to argue against and it involved an art financed by industry.

There was one person in town who had a violent break shortly after that same land agent gave a presentation to city council about a gas tax to fund the arts.

The man who had fainted at the city hall meeting during the presentation started shooting up an old farming combine and ended up murdering his best friend. People said the normal retired guy had a departure from reality of some sort.

Was it related to the strange meetings at city hall, the ones not open to the public?

And who was driving the truck that spilled the crude at the back of my ranch?

There is someone who has a dark myth in their genes and who does lots of tinkering behind the scenes every day. That person said madness and homelessness are the only alternative to allowing a pipeline, and some people seemed to agree.

o

Thing is, everything was good, and probably gooder than it had ever been, which was strange because at the same time, it was all so terrible.

Reminds me of back when Innisfree was a place of family for me: the honey, the young'ns. Everything seemed dandy until little Tommy and Brandy and Mummy started getting the lung problems and the colours on their tongues, which we thought was flesh-wasting disease at first but, turned out to be something that was more of a poisoning than a disease. They had to go to the southern cities to get treated for respiratory inflammation. Looking at it from each angle now, it's probably a good thing they never returned.

The memories are like bagged weasels, though. Can see the dust rising off roads. Feeling of drought comes right to mouth. A well dry of tears, baked-in ducts.

Can hear Tommy coughing and Brandy coughing too, and Mummy wheezing like I'd never heard before. I can taste their leaving like cough syrup forced down the throat on a spoon. But they knew, and I knew, that I had to remain with the herd and keep Innisfree going against that which threatened us.

o

At the beginning of the end of the normal times—must have been somewhere in the mid-season, when the wildflowers produce nectar in the valley and the three-spined stickleback fishes swim into the shallows to feed on house flies—Memily came over and told me something had happened to Dan-the-Man.

He's been going out there, Memily said, shaking as she told me about his obsession.

Dan went out there the first time because he saw something in the alders, she continued.

Her story reminded me of something I had seen as well. The stooped things that would catch my eye in the sag and pattern of what is just out of sight where the fields meet the mountains.

Her and Dan were doing some welding, Memily said. They both saw this red light in the willows in the field, and a sort of moose-like head behind the art barn. And the barn light illuminating a figure standing on his tiptoes with his arms raised up as if a trick had just been performed.

Dan's been quiet and spooked lately, Memily said. He just went to take a nap, and you know. Weird. He's doing physical stuff nonstop usually. So he grabbed the rifle from the closet and went back there. It was taller than him, he said, and you know how puffed up Dan is. It was taller than Dan. He chased it and chased it.

And?

Memily's brow furrowed.

He chased it over to your property, Inkster. Said he chased it into the field over in the corner of the property where the accident happened. Sorry to mention it.

Dan said it was always ahead of him, and its head looked like a rusted water pail with antlers made of exhaust pipes. It was windy that night. The grasses were taller than Dan's head and blowing about. He was scared, even with the rifle, once he got into the high grasses. And so he came back. I had followed him part of the way and it startled him when he saw me. He was sweating and the sweat still hasn't gone away. He's been going out there every night to try to find what it was. And to shoot it if he has to.

And what about the red light? I asked.

Turned out it was just a plain old man who was lost, crazy enough, said Memily, shaking her head because she was mad she'd forgotten about that part of the story.

For some reason, he was spinning around with arms upraised, like this, in the light me and Dan use to illuminate the *many i's.*

He was trying to find Cheryl's property, Memily said.

I'm a curious man, and after me and Memily and Artsy Boy watched a couple Humphrey Bogart films at Artsy Boy's, I decided to go see what Cheryl was doing because I hoped zhe was okay and also wanted to poke about a bit and connect some dots.

Cheryl wasn't home, but the next day while fixing fence way out yonder at the very backmost parts of the property, and hoping to get a glimpse of any saboteurs in the bush, I spotted what at first I saw as two frumpyish gals emerge from the creaky doors of a rusty pickup, each in black-and-red plaid and work pants and gumboots. One with a joint between her lips.

Didn't recognize it was Cheryl Hill because zhe wasn't prettied up in drag—but more of a tomboy outfit, which was even more confusing than zher usual crosshatch ways. Zhe and zher friend were shovelling gravel into the back of their pickup—grind of shovels on wet stones—apparently poaching Gasbro gravel, because that was near the new right-of-way. The company uses lots of high-quality gravel in the trenches to rest the pipelines on before covering them. The joint magically disappeared when the transtomboys saw me approach, but I told them not to worry, I wouldn't snitch to border patrol about any potential grow-op the joint might have alluded to.

I asked them, Are your husbands home making soup?

Oh, you are so funny, Cheryl chuckled.

What are tomdykes doing out here in this distant pipe land, if you don't mind me asking. And what's the gravel for?

Someone is paying us to collect this gravel for them. Good money for a little grunt work.

And the less gravel it will be to go into that wound they're stabbing through to the coast, said Cheryl's friend.

Oh yes. The pipeline. We're going to dyke the pipe, Cheryl added.

Lesbos them Gasbros, I said.

Perhaps, but what's it to you? What do you know about female desire, please, Inkster? You are the only farmer without a wife in the Hellenic world.

Cheryl's friend stuck her shovel in the gravel hard. Yeah, zhe said.

I have to make a long *hmmm*, like I'm chewing the challenge over, even though the answer's a cinch.

Seeing to a woman's desire, you see, I say out the corner of my beard, is like tending to several beach fires at the same time. You got to have a fire fighter's understanding of the erotic flame, also the arsonist's finesse, to keep the many fires burning together towards a blaze.

Hey, not bad, elk daddy. Cheryl's friend seemed satisfied with my answer.

Keep lovin' all da time, remember now, I said.

Then I winked at Cheryl, nodded, then kept following the perimeter of the fence, thinking how lively life in Enderbee is, how some of the openness that comes with the city influence is making the country just plain more fun. Some don't like the new sex talk and sarcasm, but I find it a funny alternative to innocence.

And I had something else to mull over now too: how I saw what looked like a pipe bomb sticking out from under the back seat of their pickup truck. Gotcha, I thought.

Hey, I shouted into the gravel pit: Have you two seen anything? Anything funny?

Just your ass crack when you turned around, Inkster, shouted Cheryl's friend.

o

The next day, after brushing the elks and herding the ones that already have their antlers cut to the "haircut complete corrals," and also picking burrs out of some of their coats and ticks off their hides, I took time to give thanks for being able to do tasks related to the love that is natural between the species.

I was moseying along the banks of Lethe out of the fungus-smelling underwood where the herd was shading from heat and it was one of those very pleasant moments that makes me think, ah, Innisfree.

But there's a growing noise. And soon the noise presents itself, and it's a truly huge vessel or ship, or just plain old big boat, floating along the waters of Lethe, right down the deep middle of that river distinguished by its green fathomlessness and blue flowerings in the boil of currents.

At first I thought it was a steamship from the days of yore, because of what looked like turning paddlewheels churning up the already tumultuous currents, but then I realized it was coils of pipe, a rotating spindle, the bendable pipe falling in circles underwater, and as I came out onto the river bar I could see the Gasbro logo: a stag with green eyes set on the image of a gas canister. They stole that idea from me, but I do not resent them for it.

The company is laying pipes onto the bottom of Lethe now. They uncoil the pipe off the boat, and let it fall through the currents onto the silt at the bottom, and the bottom-feeders like the white sturgeon wonder what is happening, and their nervous bodies don't squeeze the eggs proper.

Hi, shouted the man with a buzz cut and sunglasses that looked like dragonfly eyes, who I recognized from town.

Hello, I hollered to the man, who stuttered in my memory.

I wondered if he knew he was standing on Shaman Rock.

We're going underwater. Submersible supertube, he said. It's in line with the economic plans of the district. The onward and upward of development left margin to right margin, and we have the subsurface rights, left margin to right margin, don't forget.

o

Steep slopes and a moon that could give you laser eye
surgery, it's so sharp round the edges. Was out there with
Memily and Cheryl on a walk when, gosh darn it, there he
is again, Mars Ares. That's his name, I told them, excited.
He's the one who dances in the barn light. Except this
time he's dressed like a pilot. Armed Forces stripes and
combat boots. Could see him up there, larger than life in
the bubble cockpit of some rocketeer's plane. Well, I'll be
damned if they haven't been installing the pipes over top
of my property using perpetual helium to float the pipe.
Look at the Aircrane lifting the coil, the floating bobbers
up there too.

SCADA systems link everything, said Memily, with remote sensor signals from microwave conductors on the
top of the most distant peaks.

o

Nights swing into days, moon into sun again. The morning, the afternoon, the evening, the water, the coffee, the orange juice—all these are pendulums swinging about us, said the person with an elk puppet at a community drama event, who looked like other guys I have seen around.

Dan Assange

SUMMARY: Environmental website designer. Works on mysterious global contracts. Came up from Squashington, which is squished under PC Columbia. Nature's Common-Law spouse of Memily.

DESCRIPTION: Washboard-y stomach, blocky head.

ALIASES: Dan-the-Man, Big Guy, Warbler (web), Chunksister (web)

o

Another day, Mars Ares approached the property with a
priest in outdoorsman robes.

Me and Samson were doing some hoof clippings when
we saw him on the right-of-way they are building. Hey!
Hey there! What the? Letting go of the elk legs we were
lifting, we made our way over.

Mars, what are you doing now?

We are consecrating one of the tubes along here, said
Mars—a blessing, in fact. Someone has been disturbing
the route.

Samson speaks up about this: No one is keen on a re-
ligion that sees humans and their developments as more
holy than animals and that doesn't see the land as having
spirits that go between art and life.

Never mind that, said Mars. We are also missing several tonnes of the fine gravel.

And as far as the gravel, I told him, there was someone
who drove out of town with a whole load of it, said he was
going all the way to Florida.

Yeah, said Artsy Boy, nobody around here would steal
that gravel because it comes from the quarry up Lethe
way . . .

The priest looked at us with dismay, as if a gross mis-
understanding had transpired.

Then Mars, who looked for a second like Chuck D
from the Happy Mines, sneered.

This man's name is Franciscan Bob, said Mars, patting
his monk on the shoulder of the waterproof gown. He is

present in this pleasant scene to preach to the pipe, that it come alive like a vein. Now, Mr. Inkster, Mr. Samson. Please . . . we respected your farm and are building our system around it, even going so far as to completely reengineer our designs and use the cursed river as a road. You are on the right-of-way. Please . . . Go get back to accusing your neighbours of doing poor business and of tampering with prosperity, you old fuddies. Really . . .

The elk all poked their noses through the brush, sniffing to see if I had more apples with me.

Not really knowing how to respond to rotten folk, we left at that point.

You can't do that in here, you can't do that kind of blessing, I muttered as I walked back into the herd, Samson trailing behind me with his video camera.

o

Late the next morning, after sleeping on the hay bales, me and Samson went together into a nearby village to see about getting another kind of pipe consecration and also a cure for the rashes.

The pipe carrier's face was pulpy as rained-upon mud, much like mine, and he joked around with us about what it meant to be traditional. Like always, he was game to help out, as I would help him out too. Though sometimes he would even help out in return for nothing.

Eh, he said, smiling. You take this land from us, now they try to take this land from all of us.

The pipe carrier rubbed the tobacco, rolled and squeezed it in the shafts of his palms. Then he spoke the local language as he smeared it along the side of the pipeline.

Inkster, why not come to the bone healer's too, said the pipe carrier after we had consecrated the pipeline to counteract what Mars and the monk had done yesterday.

Walked quite a ways with the pipe carrier, through Memily's field, through the Carlyles' and Cheryl's fields, along the rough path through the lines of grey beaten trunks, opening and closing the wire gates on our way. Waving when waving was due, at first to a neighbour and then to the half-alive things we saw staggering along the banks of the river.

The pipe carrier raised the loose thatch gate that was on top of an earthen hill halfway up one of the ridges. Geez, it's like an imposter's hill, I thought.

Pit lodge, my friend, said the pipe carrier. Traditional, ha ha.

Down the ladder into the underground lodge. People, both white and native and a bit mixed like most of us are, dressed in Enderbee regalia. I was shocked to see the bone healer up on a high bed made of stacked cedar. Lying covered by a button blanket, an earthy heat warming the whole place that smelled like fields.

Shortly after we got inside, the pipe carrier's brother showed up, dressed in a suit still because he had to come quick from the notary office.

What is the muskrat prophet saying, I asked pipe carrier. I could see the corners of his eyes were teary.

The pipe carrier whispered into my ear about the bone healer: This bone healer is the last in the long line of muskrat prophets who have all been saying that the end of the world is nigh.

And then I had to ask him: Was there never hope?

He is the last in a long line of important Big Names who predicted the end of the world and now he is dead.

What do you think, the pipe carrier's brother said, having overheard.

But what does end of the world mean?

That is what we are trying to figure out, the pipe carrier whispered hurriedly. In the meantime, the bone healer gave me this baggy. I said goodbye to him. Even on his death bed, he wants to heal.

The pipe carrier handed me a small glass jar with some greasy stuff in it.

It's made with spruce sap and beeswax, he said, in fact beeswax you gave us a long time ago. There was so much of it, Inkster, we thought there was no way . . . but here we are, years later, and well . . . Anyway, go wild. Your rash won't know what hit it.

Prophets always want a cut of the doomsday profits, that's what I was thinking as I watched the Enderbeeites come up out of the lodge one by one and throw some food as offerings into a bonfire.

But then the pipe carrier started talking more at length. Saying that there are two lines of prophets. What we just saw was the end of the muskrat healer's line.

What then? I said.

Depends on how the next thing is translated, said the pipe carrier. Some call them head expanders, others say skull crushers. So now that the last of the muskrat prophets has passed with this ceremony, they are waiting for the next thing, and they don't know if it will be a head expander or a skull crusher.

What about another bone healer?

Yes, said the pipe carrier, a bone healer is a possibility. Let us hope.

o

Summary of the summaries

These are some of us people of Enderbee and the write-ups I do to keep my illiteracy at bay. Are the people out of jobs the ones who are pissed off, or is it the people who like their land so much and have seen the damage develop from the beginning?

Nobody likes to be infiltrated, occupied, run through by metal conduit. So it seems it is not a question of who did, but maybe who didn't do it.

●

Winter now, winter on blowy day, trackless white flakes of sky. Frosted roads lead forward or backward. Off-road invisible. Investigators come and gone with their rumours of reward. A momentary freeze on memory. Only two directions. Forward or backward. Backward hits a nerve, so reverts to forward. One event interlocks with another. What must be must be. There is no agency, just the agentless placement of blocks in a line. An offer and an acceptance denied. Grammar trots straight according to the rules. The animals have spoken, cloven grammar and forked words.

o

In the winter, the summer takes on an ideal and real nice place in my mind. I will sit on the edge of the squeaky spring bed and feel the warmth of past times from before the sun getting so hot, back when the breeze would come and all was good.

I have seen an elk eating flowers before in that sun, all those petals flapping out between its giant rat-like front teeth, I remember it now—its furry neck craned from one patch of flowers to another—Wild Lupines, Nodding Trilliums, Slender Lady's Tresses—the flowers turning into their normal names then their scientific ones, right out of Samson's plant book—*Lupinus perennis, Trillium cernuum, Spiranthes lacera gracilis*—then lying again as plain petals on the grass. An elk came close enough, but I could see no number tag on its ear; it was no Hyperion, it was a free elk, one that was a distant son of the Hyperion and Mnemosyne breeding stock that escaped and bred in the Free Lands . . . it's head lowered so its world-reflecting eye was parallel to my own. I work so hard being relaxed on the ranch (elks pretty much look after themselves) that I don't have the most dramatic dreams when I do call it a night. That's why last night was so strange, how the elk chewed dandelions and then the colour of the flower absorbed the head of the elk in a halo. In the drelkam, the whole elkhead was moving slow, aglow. That's when I heard the voice of the elk—like Hank from the baseball field. Hypnotized I felt by that chew-chewing jaw, that up-and-down outfielder motion . . . "*Mmm*, there are numbers in these flowers, *mmm,*" and chewed more, swinging its neck and antlers from flower to flower. "*Mmm,* left margin to right margin right margin to left margin ... there are numbers in these flowers, *mmm,* great huge numbers, left margin to right margin, numbers too big to work with, right margin to left margin ... Keep getting lost in these deep numbers, *mmm,* and forgetting the fact that my blivets hurt, that my calculation machine hurts, that my stumps are cut and bleeding . . . But there are numbers and there are bombers and there are pendulums of love in these flowery margins. And there is pain." The elk buck-tooths its words . . .

I wake up. My pillow is wet from tears and saliva.

It does make their antlers funny-forked, cutting them all off like that, don't you think, Mr. Inkster?

The elk begin to appraise me differently over morning feed, with pained squints and distrust.

o

And then comes spring out of the rot thaw, transforming from the newlywed landscape of yesterday—midnight iris open, planet conscious. That's how Artsy Boy describes it. Farmhouse window framing field. On the wing, nighthawk feeds on flying ants out in my pastures. Lit pink-orange and panther-black. Moon rays dramatize the willows where the elk forage. In the foothills behind, gas stacks flare their excess in floating gulps of yellow fog. What out that frame do my tired eyes conjure or see—a three-legged, fork-headed thing staggering underneath the ledge of the trees, bent-backed, dipping in and out of sunken boulders that hump the field. Nature's perfume, the threaded wind, and some chemical woven through those winds that smells like floor cleaner. Night-bird calling relaxes me. The figure holds a still ear between the willows and alders, listening to the chime of a key clicking in the night, and I sink back down into my covers to sleep again at the same time as the figure levitates away into the fields and the nighthawk sticks its head back under its wing, lashes fluttering over pomegranate-coloured eyes one third the size of its head. When I sleep, too, I see in a drelkam the torso of that person float through the grain in the direction of the mountain, and all the elk, on those nights, seem to migrate across Innisfree from the plain into the forest.

o

Another eruption took out a wellhead a few kilometres from Innisfree, which caused a sour gas leak. Sour gas comes from the earth bowels where Lethe flows up from. It is invisible and scentless and lethal like death itself. No country for old elk farmers. What the heck, eh? When I was chasing down a Hyperion for antler removal the other day, a gas stack flared so loud it made both me and the elk leap off the slough bank into the reeds. Hurting my old man body in a bad way, and scaring the bejesus out of the Hyperion.

I'd prefer to just sit all day on the porch in bare feet tickled by the wind on the fringe of my calluses and bunions.

It's the most neatest thing. How everyone's anxieties seem to fall asleep when the western song frog sings (right margin to left margin).

But these lulls mean trouble is a-brewing. Trouble, trouble. No country for an old elk farmer like me.

o

It's all about the input you put in and the output you get from that. Robotillers punch pores in the ground for the petro fertilizer to absorb into. Thousands of workers came here for jobs, and the working class is now the ruling class. Some come for the agricultural crews that paint plants with water that is like plastic in that it will slowly drip on the plants when it melts in the sun. Farmbots plant fig trees and sometimes a timed shadow is activated that covers half the visible horizon. We can see all this from Charybdis Ridge on the tour of the ranch. Supercombines sit side by side in big parking bays next to the farmhouses made of combed aluminum. Blue spray shoots from spouts, a nitrogen booster to the fertilizer pellets. The flare stacks from the gas look like lighters held high at an olden-day concert, while the compressor stations that suction oil or force the gas and other liquids through the pipes look like huge bongs—according to Artsy Boy, that is. This view isn't a view we steer the wagon tours towards, unless the visitors really want to see.

o

Samson's book collection grows and shrinks depending on how many he's lending out or borrowing, and he always bitches that he never gets them back.

Kind of like the layout of Memily's field, I mean how the art is always changing. She takes it apart and reassembles it all the time.

Nights swing into days, moon into sun again. The afternoon nap, the evening snack, the coffee with chrome surface, the cherry pie, the cube of butter—all these are pendulums swinging about us, said the person with a puppet of an elk at the community drama event.

We've already started planning for the fall harvest, autumn apple cider tours. Life goes on. Concern about the big explosion has settled down, as it seems the saboteur is an amateur. We walk the fields feeling safer because of this knowledge. Except for the vapourized farm dog incident. I will miss Little Orange.

Little Orange, I yelled out.

But it's too late, the signal light is blinking under the drone propellers, so we know it has the dog clocked. The particle ray zaps down in a corkscrew of razor-sharp light.

And all that's left of our farm dog is a puff of dust and a burnt patch in the grass.

STAY CLEAR OF THE EXPLOSION SITE. GASBRO HAS CLOSED THE AREA. ALL INTERLOPERS WILL BE VAPORIZED.

The pie, the moon, the waving wall of trees on the hill, the morning, the noon siesta, the evening, the people sitting around in the shed. They are forming what looks like playdough into the shape of elks with one red eye blinking.

Fury of ancients propels action's sail, twisting passion fire gimlets through water wheels of burning myths of unsettling the settlers. Every contraction is an action dictated by a myth dictator. Fallen ones decree what the bird has elk has. This is what the great ecosystem of the Can'tadian Northwest has decreed. This is what Ares says must be. Rage against rage. Titan against Olympian. No passion, no emotion. A decision made and stuck with. Left margin to right margin. C-4 Plastico. Duffle bag stuffed. Any doubt is dispelled by the Stellar's Jay, nothing except a blank mist in the heart. Right margin to left margin. To secure second detonation device. Up to four. Timed to go off sequentially. At bottom of waterbody swim swim underwater Beowulf and Iron Grendel swum swum down to the bottom where sunken frog bellies levitate, down to the letter bottom. Persephone down down Persephone. Skin beats benthic. Persephone weedbed hair drowned towns figures moat floating. The Queen's name spoken means impact, concussion, rape. Locate pipe at bottom of river fighting the currents as mighty scaled torpedo. Dolphins deactivating bombs on the ocean floor human activating a bomb at top of ocean floor terrestrial.

o

The elk have been acting real strange, boy, and it was the biggest of them, Hyperion I, the oldest one, that Dan saw the other day when he was searching for that thing that is always bugging him out the corner of his eye.

What torment drew me into the marginal areas after I heard Memily's story of Dan's obsession, as if the whimper of something out there, a run-over animal noise translated into "I am lame, come save me with a bullet". Around the edges of an open area, the elk came out of the holes in the blankets of mist, and though I held out a paper bag of dried pineapple, they kept glaring at me and tramped forward. Never had their chests looked bigger. The full size of them is only apparent when close up. Snorting and coming at me with their branchless heads lowered. And then they raised their necks and bugled, and stomped the earth as they prepared to charge. Their knees breaking through an old fence and smashing fireweeds, and I had to drop and curl and roll like a man lit on fire. Could feel their hot breath snorted wet on my neck as I fell and they pounded me with hoof and punctured me with whatever barbs remained of their antlers.

Marlowe Says Pipeline Plot No Delusion

—5 April 2038—

"We are increasing the reward to $500,000 for any information leading to the arrest of the pipeline bomber." So said CEO of Gasbro, Chase Beefrude, in a public statement Sunday morning.

This amount matches the PDNQ's increase of the standard police award bounty from $10,000 to $500,000 and could be a sign of desperation, said a source.

The second bombing in just over a month rocked a gas line near Byzantium, indicating that the bomber could be working on both sides of the West-Central border.

Catfish Marlowe of the PDNQ downplayed fears that this could be an inside job carried out by border patrol.

"The screening process for all provincial borders is extreme. What we are looking at here is most likely an international plot of some kind, but focused within PC Columbia. Paranoia is no longer a delusion; it is the substance of society and the cause of our decline."

Stay tuned for more up-to-the-second updates on the *Troutsource* blog, and continue reading the prose poem feeds through *Podview*.

Derrida Bloom has written a *piece* of scholarly poetry about his own attempt to trace some of the mythological themes of the satellite feed of the prose poem progression:

It is my belief that these action prose poems were footsteps from Greece to Enderbee. An early art terrorist had rocked the Hippocrene where the muses were imprisoned in statues by industrial magistrate Zeus, blowing them free with blasts of an early form of explosive called Greek Fire. From the shores at the bottom of Mount Olympus, we can posit that the creative titans and the escaped muses sailed away o-way. Aeneas was on the boat for a time; Quetzalcoatl was on the boat; for a moment or two, it was the Ship of Fools; in another incarnation, two of each species were said to be on that boat; the boat is named Pequot; the Ghost; or it divides in three and becomes the Niña, the Pinta, and the Santa Maria. But then it became the ivory-hulled vessel of the titans, then cedar dugout coated in mist and sleet. The boat a topology of myth. The map a surreal array of sections of absence and native talent. At that point the boat arrived in the Northwest of Can'tada, it had become a train full of settlers; a Haida sea vessel; a canoe guided with J-stroke, old ways faded from the paddlers' hands. Then it was a steam engine. A gunpowder keg rolled too close to the coal furnace; somewhere near the island of Lilburn, the ship with the ancients and the microbial muses was hit with an accidental detonation. Fragments of the living and inanimate contents of the vessel got washed down through the currents, some muses were lost in the deep dark and some gods escaped to shore. God-relations melted into animal-relations; lovers in the myth became scattered fawns, footprints the shape of divided hearts in the bright mud. A decomposing filmstrip, even the poems fallout from some sort of meltdown at the core of words.

o

One ranch hand said it was too bad I had been ejected from my saddle into the briar and got beaten up too bad to come into town, but I told her it could have been worse. You shoulda seen Mayor Timothy, she told me.

She said Mayor Tim got hypnotized with all the pictures they flashed on a screen made of stitched-together beehive, and by cracking nutmeg sticks near his nose. They got the mayor to take that silver dress shirt off, to comb his chest hair with an oversized brush, and reach a hand down his pants suggesting to him it was the Klondike and he was after gold nuggets.

Well har har, sniffle snort! I told the ranch hand, a dark-faced lass with twisty hair in a checkered gingham scarf.

I told her the hypnotist used to be the gym teacher at Enderbee middle school. He's always had a knack for getting people to take their shirts off. And he used a chunk of orange agate shaped like a peach and told folks to hold it, tight or loose depending on whatever quality he saw in the person, and said to concentrate on the objects of their desire.

Apparently this is a new hypnotist with new stuff, actually, the ranch hand said. No peach rock, he actually used a decommissioned hand grenade for what he called telemetry, or haptic divination. Big word hypnotist I s'pose.

Oh? I said.

Yes. He said that he'll come to your house to do a personal show. Wouldn't that be fun? He could hypnotize some elk.

My house? My elk?

Joking, Inkster. Buuttt . . . the new hypnotist did have some drinks with us after his show and the booze got him loose-lipped. Said he knew how to do a trick with an elk.

Oh?

Yeah, you know how an elk has four stomachs—one that stores the food it swallows, like you yourself told us, Inkster, and the other three stomachs for breaking the food down. Well the new hypnotist said he's working on a trick to hide something in that fourth stomach.

Strange that any magician would reveal their tricks, I said.

●

Final, fifth device secure. Stick in aerial scramblers to stun shut-down sensors. Feel along pipe for groove to facilitate latching. Normax detonator. Summer flowers. Disguised as welder. Reach with left arm 'round cement taper node. Knee ground in gravel. Won't fasten properly to strut. Wiggle thighs sideways, readjust centre of balance. Reach device 'round steel wall of buttress this time. Cluclonk goes magnet. Bingo. Grab remote from pocket, check signal, retreat into alpine, again check signal. Bingo. Now wild tiger lilies into the lupines into the spiraea into the aphid-covered brush that has migrated everywhere the pilgrimage of plants disappear to reappear grasshopper fiddles. Mouth mandibles owl clicks its beak dwam of evening. Ha. Boo. Ha. Move. Ha. A green-robed pathway. Lily pads. Wading. Security in their mud wagon watching power erotica. Byzantium aglow with its shiny night armour beaten into shape by the desires of the townspeople, a bear into alder a seal into water symbol into meta-roar.

o

I mean, there was, oh there most certainly was some things that people were doing that I knew of and kept my lips pursed about. Such as the hefty neodymium magnets hid along the path where Gasbro was putting their pipelines in them riparian areas. Magnets buried strategywise so soon as the cranes lowered the steel pipes they would get jerked away from their linear bearing and become dented and twisted on surrounding land features. There are old mining holes here and there, and it is within these caverns that the magnets are marshalled. But that is not something I am involved in, though I would certainly like to know who is, and I think I might have a notion. Let us go that way, just over yonder.

o

Memily calls over the black wire fence into the grey light of my day. The strands of her hair playing tag with her summer moles, and her dimpled eyes squirrelled away in the tunnels of her flappy sun hat. Her highland skin white and vulnerable in the streaks of light through predominant black shadows. What, I wonder, is she doing in this landscape of death tones.

Inkster, how are you? I keep seeing you pacing around over there.

Okay I guess, Memily.

Looks like that rash you were talking about has gone away.

Yup . . . yup . . . That's a good thing, I suppose, because if it was flesh-wasting disease, I reckon you'd have it too. I don't usually like talking over fences, though, you know, Memily.

I like the old-fashioned farmer etiquette, Mr. Inkster. I've noticed, she says, that you are entering your masterwork, just like they said you would. You know, your project to live with a herd for a year, and finally extend the boundaries of your fence into the mountains where the valleys are and the streams that would make Innisfree self-sufficient.

While she's talking, she undoes the wire latch of a gate. We stand together in a patch of shade on her side.

I can't see what's happening anymore, I say. The science of it escapes me. All I can do is sing my second song . . . "My favourite animal's womb has become a tomb. Where

114

not life but death is born in skeletal bloom . . ."

She puts her arms around me and squeezes me kindly. She was there by the shore in the gathering ceremony when we released the elkchild into the river currents to be taken away.

I like your song about loving all the time better, Jeffery, she says, hinting that mourning for the lost calf has run its course. Besides, you know it's your masterwork when you can feel it falling apart, can't see it, and you have to hold on tight. I know that from art, not science. I'm a welder in disguise, Inkster, when I see you moving through your fields with the hay and the alfalfa, the elk circle you, you know that, they can tell you are on solid ground. Don't let bombs and miscarriages throw you too much.

A welder disguise, eh Memily?

Well, figuratively, Jeffery, figuratively. We're not talking antler weight here.

She looks away into the fields, as if searching for inspiration in the distance, and my eyes follow her gaze out there.

What was I like when I first came here, Memily?

You were like a jitterbug. Your pace has slowed. More amble and pause, not point and click.

She asks me if I want to come talk to her while she works on her art down at the shop.

What are you working on now, Memily?

She has changed a little as I speak, the shadows catch a different angle of her personality.

People of Byzantium made from scrap metal, and other stuff from the dump. It used to be that we were simply pluses and minuses, but now we are strings of pluses and series of minuses, so it's harder to attach. That's what these melted latches are, the metal latches that hold us back. Like the ones that block you and Dan-the-Man from ever being friends. Or from me moving on from my sadness at never having a child, which was just an instinct fading like a star.

Memily hammers the face of one of her sculptures with the mallet, denting in a cheekbone, straightening a minus.

I am doing another sculpture about complicity too, she says.

Her eyes say hi to me from under the flapping brim.

o

This is what I got from my talk with Memily:

There are many kilometres of fence around Innisfree, so that means lots of fence to sit on. Thing is, when you lift your ass off the fence, you end up on one side or the other. I would prefer not to be on either side. You see, a fence sitter has the advantage of being able to reason with people on either side, and to bring the escape rope down to lift everyone away from all fences altogether, which would be the great ecstatic forever, wouldn't it now, Artsy Boy?

Not Your Usual Suspects

—1 May 2038—

A bomb plot targeting the heavy production zone of the Rockies-Always-the-Rockies has stirred up local Enderbee politics enough to cause the current mayor to step down.

The Mayor of Enderbee, Timothy Pleaser, who has until a recent recessional dip taken an anti-bitumenlite position, has resigned after expressing public disgust with everyone involved in the conflict and being slammed for not taking a side for or against. This leaves the small town of Byzantium without a strong leader, says the head of the regional district, Anne Carters.

The temporary incumbent mayor, Sam Sears, is acting on an emergency political platform aimed at liquidating Enderbee title to make it part of Cowberta, says Carters. The newly industry-wealthy of Enderbee, though they appreciate the lawlessness of their unceded treaty domain, apparently appreciate the toys afforded by savings from low tax rates even more, as a recent poll showed support of the interim mayor's plan at fifty-four percent.

"The Gasbro high-pressure pipeline is already four weeks into its accelerated construction phase at a pace of 20 kilometres per day, and the patterns of the bombings indicate a 'closing noose' pattern around the Enderbee portion of the project," Charters observed. She added that the pipeline will be completed within 10 months.

Troutsource is now at ground level with one reporter dispatched from our Cancougar newsroom trying to get a sense of the insanity. Stories of investigators tailing Byzantium residents are commonplace. Here is some of what the incredulous locals had to say.

From local resident Cheryl Hill, interviewed after we noticed her cornered by several officers at Parkwood Mall:

"Well, I'm transgender now, right, so of course they are going to think I'm linked to the criminal element. To tell you the truth, I don't give a damn, they can ask me all the questions they want—I am all ears, honey. Mayor Timothy is such a sweet man, the poor guy is being blamed for not keeping more of a lid on all the crap. They want to pin this on freaky radicals, and because they can see how beautifully freak I am, they pay extra attention to my femme nature. However, just because someone seems freak, doesn't mean they are, you dummies. I've been singled out all my life, it's all right, I have a tough hide, anyway. Spank away, baby."

Peter Bucklet, the owner of Jewelled Smithery Hardware Store:

"Asking me for name lists of everybody I've sold a bolt to, credit card statements and descriptions of clients. It's crazy. Riffling through the doodads in the discount bins. Really crazy. Sometimes buying fertilizer is just buying fertilizer, right? I mean, hello dumbnuts, if it's really the green angel investors behind this, why would they be buying their bomb ingredients here at the hardware store? They would be growing them in terrorist hothouses or some shit."

o

Innisfreers got snooped on, we sure did. I told the police about the investigations I'd been doing myself, and they said if I persevered, the money could be mine. But I told them I had no interest in that; even if I were to be successful in finding the perpetrator, I'd not accept it from them, because what I really wanted was the very knowledge about the explosive secret and to have justice come to that person or persons if they were plotting anything *really really really* bad. And besides, was I really going to tell the cops? Nu-uh. Though I am not a legal-type person, it was plain from the prose poems on *Troutsource* that the character in the poem picked up by the decoder satellite was of the bad order of weird.

When I was being investigated over at the police bureau, like all of us were, they asked me about everything I knew, which was nothing. Nobody knew anything; it was really just going through the motions. But those motions were based on corrupt and scary notions, I soon discovered.

You see, there was a *Troutsource* journalist hanging around. Finally disarmed owing to the news outlet's reputation for being reasonable, I decided heck, why not, it was okay to give the journalist some details, because details are locked away and hard to come by for all of us, which must be especially frustrating for someone in his line of work. And he had something to give me in return, not that I believe every good turn must be met with a favour.

He asked me about the community dynamics, and I told him what I could.

And then he dropped the bombshell.

Whaaaaat????? I said. How do you know they think it might be me?

Listen, said the journalist—who looked like an everyday person and not how you'd think a journalist should or would look—I will give you the old list of persons of interest that someone leaked from the police database. But only if you show me the Other barn.

Well, sure, I said, I would like to take a journalist like you to do that.

But I had to tell him there was little substance to my story. The story didn't have much in the way of legs, in other words, or, harhar, antlers.

Well, Inkster, don't forget that you are on the list, said the journalist.

Reference	Name	Lead	History
1 3	The Carlyle family	Radical Christian family known to possess an arsenal of monkeywrenching paraphernalia.	Explosives seized in 2026 from property, no permit.
2 1	Cheryl Hill	Erratic behaviour, unstable identity, proximity to conduits.	Charged in Cowberta for siphoning gas from Gasbro trucks.
3 2	Samson Huckleberry	Radical drifter type, avant-garde film, proximity to conduits.	Several arrests for illegal breeding of livestock and suspected history of bestiality.
4	Dan Assange, AKA "Dan-the-Man"	Emails tracked through trans-provincial servers to enviroleak watchdog groups.	Previously investigated for data leaking during Borderland Reformation.
5	Stranger who goes by "Mars Ares," real name unknown. Untraceable.	Impersonated a Borderland agent, potential connection to human programming groups.	Deep web indicates profile of typical border-drifting info-gatherer.
6	Memily Assange	Political artist who perverts reality. Knowledge of welding and compression fittings.	Perceived within Enderbee as too peace-loving to be a bomber, however might be complicit.
7	Jeffery Inkster	Elk farmer with sadistic tendencies. Proximity to conduits.	Knowledge-holder. Potential informant and enabler.

o

The farm tours weren't going so well that Year of the Secret, on account of the rains, and on account of the explosions rocking the community and on account of the suspicions. The winter had been longer again, and the ground was too muddy for the wagon wheels to roll proper on the first day.

People still wanted some therapy, they did, but fewer came for the wagon tours, indeed they didn't.

I swear, going to Byzantium, seemed the hypnotist's business was the most flourishing of all.

I was in town to check on matters related to the maintenance and permitting of Innisfree, involving a duotang with paperwork and such, and to purchase wire and posts, with just me and a couple trained elk to haul it all back.

After passing the hypnotist's big studio on Main St., I noticed a person sitting at the window of the hot drink shop with his hand spread over his face. Kind of like a latte manikin, I thought. And there, on his shirt, was a picture of flowers and a bird, a Tweety Bird.

And the funniest thing happened to me, everything went dim, then totally dark. I got knock-kneed, had to grope outward, find something to balance on.

I hadn't gone on a good bender since hard times, so it seemed odd I'd be losing my vision. But my hands found a pole to grasp and I just stood there for a few moments, and slowly, the deeper I breathed, the more light got back into my eyes and then I could see what was on the pole.

Withdrew my hands right quick, and looked around to

make sure nobody was seeing this.

You see, there was another one of those threat letters stuck against the pole staring up at me.

I whipped around and looked back into the hot drink shop. The man with the hand spread over his face and the Tweety Bird shirt, he was still there, looking down through the empty space between his fingers at something on the table I couldn't see. I swung back to gaze at the letter again.

Be finally warned. The town has chosen unwisely not to honour our wishes, so now it is time for Gasbro to meet the real Bone Crusher. By the time you read this letter the fate of many lives will be at risk. The only way you can stop this event from escalating is by shutting down all Scylla Ridge operations IMMEDIATELY as well as Site C463 adjacent to the headwaters of the Microchip and Lethe. What has been so cunningly dealt by SKULL CRUSHER so far is but a fraction of the REAL power of BRAIN ANNIHILATOR. If you hesitate for a MOMENT longer we will make the decision for you.

o

Back at Innisfree, the rain starts on the 1950s cars that look like black top hats floating down the liquid driveway.

Yes indeed, Artsy Boy has got an unholy glow about him, like a Spartan. He's shaved his head in those short ridges along the temples and jaw, like a North American hyena who's been to the LA barbershop, and he's making a scene at the humble elk cider sampling of Sunday evening. Kids working the old cash registers on old schoolroom desks between plum trees (part of the tour is getting involved in all aspects of the ranch and selling cider and the like), and a father belts out, ramped up by dandelion wine, belly-laughing, hurrahing: Look at Artsy Boy's big eyes and velvet antler hair, like he's turning into an elk, haw haw. Chuck D throwing a handful of straw at Dan-the-Man, gets some on Memily and Miss Primrose from the bison estate. There's Samson now juggling eggs like they were our heads, our noggin-encapsulated fates.

We're all starting to look kinda like elk, I agree, feeling somehow drawn into currents of resistance. We'll do something to stop them from putting the pipe through Tipping Point River! To expect me not to be smart, as a farmer, would be a stereotype, would it not? To expect me not to defend my land would as well. It's not like I have a webbed nose with veins that speak of cigarettes and steak, or purple wormy blockages. It's not as though I have a lump on my cheek that looks like a tit. You are turning into some ghastly pioneer, you say? Claiming I speak in "done goods" and "sump'ns" and "get at 'ers." Well, on days off at the barn dances, I dress in my best duds like the good old days, you'll see.

Shuffle them in, shuffle them out. Bucket after bucket with the new elk velvet antlers. Surgical gloves. Alembic. Manoeuvring the Hyperion into place. The sclurch sound of the saw cutting tissue muffles a voice. Hey there, buddy. Buddy, what you doing, I thought you were driving me to ball practice? Hey! Then twenty pound plastic baggies full of elk powder trucked up from Cancougar. Buyers overseas. Get the ranch hands to sieve it into twist-top bags. It's fucking gold, says one of the ranch hands.

o

Heard a Mnemosyne keening in the knocking pine trees. We tried to ease the calf out. But Mnemosyne's eyes rolled and she squealed, and what came out of her looked dark in my hands, a blackness as of warm blood. But it was not an elk baby born, it was a crow born, and it was not alive. It was a stillborn crow. Another elk gave birth to a live crow and we called it Baby Crow. The crow would caw in a human voice, a kid's voice. And when it did, usually another stillbirth happened soon thereafter.

●

Now. Now! It's doom time. Except for wind is over sixty clicks southwesterly. Gad dang. Heart goes boom boom chest and flick of memory, a man smiling under headache light of saloon after last call. Tweety Bird shirt. Press once, twice, enter code. But no, not work. Something scrambling the wireless relay encryption. Or dead sensor. Soggy wait in bog killed the battery. Must have. Track back. Can't think. Illusion disappearing. Identity trombone. Wahoop. Am someone am someone. Bird. Sky. Left margin to right margin right margin to left margin left margin to right margin. In the book of pain. Orphan memories once repressed. Now forget. Back along pond bank. To ditch moat. Reach around the edge again. Must feel. The feeling of being surveyed from a satellite. Watched, world's eyes on everyone. Pseudo-welder. Manually reverse-working what a welder normally would. A toggle to turn one eighth of a rotation. And a widget to depress halfway. Sound of aerosol sprayed. Tearing around the metering shed's reinforced wall. A pre-explosion. Turn run. Run like hell. Smoke consuming. Boom. Vavoom. Vacuum suck, smack shed, blow forward in wrath of flame. Insert special effects.

o

Out the kitchen window: a Hyperion, antler stumps bandaged, spooked around the side of the barn, animal inspector pursuing with a thermometer.

Those goddamn animal activist goons. They have no right. No right, I say! Third time in twenty years, each time they get nosier. This time it's the sporty inspector with the no-prisoners look, someone whose attention could bring a vicious punishment to your world, who's got the quiet power of a civil servant in charge of the guillotine, and calls herself Mae Sarrs, which rings some sort of strange bell.

Sarrs finishes testing the elk's water, doing stuff like measuring the antibiotic levels, examining the elk's living conditions and whatnot. Returns to the farmhouse where I am busy furrowing my brow and cursing.

Jeffery, this is your third notice, it's serious now. Pulls out her binder full of checklists and forms and all that.

She's come up from Cancougar, and her brand of judgmentalism is not appreciated here. Just listen to her!

Mr. Inkster, elk farming is not ecologically sound in the first place, especially the way you do it. I've said it before, and I will say it again. It's not something that the PC government has ever liked, and if there didn't exist cross-zonal laws with Cowberta, you can betcha the regional district would shut you right down (taps her pen on the pages of her assessment). The anesthetic you are currently using for the velvet antler removal is adequate; however, you will be required to upgrade your tourniquet system to a hydraulic press to block blood flow. Overall your elk look . . . well . . . sad. Probably the pain in their temples from your inhumane sawing technique executed without sufficient anesthetic. If this persists, and you don't upgrade, it could become a matter for the bureau of animal rights.

I told you about the birth problems, I spit back . . . it's the gases from all those pipes. Just smell the air out there. And look here at my hands, from petting the elks after they've been lying around near the gas stacks. Their depression is no result of mine.

Mr. Inkster, I've looked into the possible correlation between the miscarriages and the emissions as per our conversation, and also the supposed rashes. Again, the studies have found no realistic link. Poor farming practice is more likely the reason why you have seen a high incidence of stillbirth. As for rashes, well, those look like bed bug bites, probably brought into Enderbee by the transients . . . Moving on now—the condition in the velvet antler barn . . . Not good. She passes me the clipboard with the checklist on it. As you can see, the mood scale and nesting condition ratings all come out really low.

I swing the binder around, feeling it scrape against my scabby wrists. General livestock health: 2/5. Overall animal form and vigour: 2/5. Responsiveness to approach: 2.5/5.

Animal depression, Mr. Inkster. Nothing sadder than when you realize other creatures have deep emotions just like us.

Listen. This is how I live. This is how my elk live. You

come in here with your official checklists . . . You don't get it. They live a good life out here.

You can't hide this from yourself much longer.

What is she talking about. Hide what I do every day? From myself?

Oh, and one more thing.

I surrender, Mae.

You need to take the new Velvet Antler Removal Certification Program.

My dear Mae Sarrs, oh my dear . . .

But then the bohemian waxwings croon with gravelly voices, a Hyperion bugles from the Free Lands, and this makes me imagine autumnal hues come out from a pastel spout, sound-confetti of lavender, russet, aubergine, in swirls, spirals, multicolour twists. Heard it described as sounding like several flutes blown together hard like a horn.

Dan-the-Man and Memily come strolling up the road after dear Mae has departed back south.

Don't worry, brother, Dan says to me, patting my defeated shoulder with his clubbed hand. We are going to sink this complicity boat soon, we'll all clean up our acts . . . We are all, all of us, complicit.

o

To another lost Mnemosyne and the misery of being not quite here. One day the elkclockmaker snatched you, took you into the areas not mapped. The past is like a glacier, calf must be somewhere inside tapping the arctic glass with her teacup hooves. Cannot give up on the mystery— mystery along the cranberry paths on the way through the bush, not just in the clearing at the end. The forest's hurt throbs sometimes, doesn't it? Why do people hurt? That is what he asked underneath the fir tree. Under the fir tree, he wondered why nature created pain. Coughing hay bits, sunburned eyelids touched with dusty fingers, moles on my back rubbing against the sappy scales of the tree. Didn't I used to be a typical farmer with a strong wife and rosy-cheeked child, didn't I? Didn't I used to, before that, live in a wet, readerly city somewhere in Squashington? Times are strange in these regions of the rural future, and I don't blame them for never returning to a place of dying beauty. Search units come overhead looking for border-breachers, but underneath the fir tree they can't see. Under the fir tree I ask why oh why did you create pain, let me know at least that one part, or at least let me thank you for the numbness that comes when it gets too bad, at least there is that.

And Mnemosyne XVII aborted three calves in a row.

And for every abortion another bomb went off.

Held each bloody produce in my arms, cast them into the streams where the trout gulped them up. I don't like the mindless mouthings of the fish.

When you meditate on the image of the crystalline lit elk, the crystal Elkhead flickering with light—when you meditate on the sound of hooves in woods. That is the practice he started so long ways ago, underneath the fir tree. Now, under the fir tree, the sides of his head ache, and he rubs them in confusion, wondering if he bumped his head in the middle of the night.

●

A ball of flame envelopes the summer green. Wahoop! A ball of flame devours the progress of Olympian-loyal westernkind. Wahoop! Oil gushes from the torn pipes from garden hose with press of a tongue, a black hose, black water over a doll house, black tongue two packs a day. A cardinal observes from Rome, Cowberta. Whistle of bitumenlite condensing into a torrent of super-dense liquid dumped by high winds away and down, away black wave. Looming shadow made of steam liquid over turned shoulder. Black tidal wave. Dollops of burning oil flaming around their edges drop and plop smell of gas tank when nose is stuck right in. Wahoop! Wahoop! Hedge-hopper, grasshopper, rabbit jumper away. Crescent shadow of beech tree. Gasbro has fallen. Wahoop. Citadels of the barons are no longer. Wahoop. Every explosion a division and a multiplication. Mouth exploding with charcoal spittle. An umbrella of bitumenlite vavoooms over the valley. Into the forest into the forest. Arm becomes burning sceptre.

o

Memily and Dan-the-Man have created a canoe poem. A canoe that has what are apparently called verses carved through the side. The words of doubt and irony make this a leaky vessel. It's the "Canoe Called Complicity," Memily explains, as she experiences overexposure of her autumnal hair.

The words carved through the canoe—legible by the same sharp-edged light as cracks between planks of an outhouse door:

The salmon, a gagged witness to its own horror he screams
and the eco forester has destroyed more streams than
the apolitical consumer and why you hate mega dams
most while electric shaving and everyone sells out after uni
the song of the satanic preacher you fucking bloke.
Must be balanced with sinkers, what is weighted wrong
Sink as deep as darkness can, may this Canoe of Complicity go
So we can get back on course, make pancakes on a different day

The canoe is supported with a wooden block at each end, dripping biodegradable paint from cottonwood walls. Sunlight passes through letters of doubt and irony.

What's the point of this whole complicity thing, I ask Dan-the-Man.

He just looks at me.

Can't you see the poem here is about you too? he says, in an exaggerated baritone. When we launch our vessel into the lake and try to paddle, people like you are going to sink it, Mr. Inkster.

Since when did Dan-the-Man get such a hate on for me—or is it man love with rusted hinges just grating against the shoulder?

●

Sound what the whack, sound what the clack, seems to happen smack. Tear off welding disguise with one free arm. Over shoulder some mauve sea image, trilobites of sparks. Twin pipeline twisted into venom array. Charge two three four five in tandem—geysers spurting squid leagues high with each flame ball, arrows of blazing gunk falling over Byzantium, globular torpedoes. Holy shit. Was supposed to be a warning. Just one segment. But night bird calls. Right margin to left margin. Forget. Manic excitement overwhelms, the laughter of the completion, the having gotten it done, the wicked excellence, the exhilaration. Hopping bouncing running; cackling and spitting blood so vital. Trip. Grab for something to stabilize. Swing of an arm miss of the target. Fall, rise, keep scampering. Can't. Can't push, arm groping through the earth, touches hair touches hair that is laughter. A gauntlet grabs hold of hand in some underground salute. No left arm no more. Dark ages. Absence. Where? Can't lift. Arm of fire. Ghost pressure on chest. Attempt to breathe. Breath. On knees. Prostrate. Hair burn. Tarred-in lungs. Stumbling farther. Smoked legs. Smoking body. Steaming body. Stumble through rosy moon shadows. Known rock formations—find them, hide. Hunker. Need to just. Find a deeper. Shadow. In which. To pass out. Plump raindrop snuffs candle. Puff of smoke from rock ring of charcoals. Asleep with armless stump pointed upwards.

o

Them action poems that I first saw in the paper and on *Troutsource* have found their way onto law enforcement websites. I don't recall whether it was one of the ranch hands started showing them to me or whether I ended up there myself, but they sure aren't the kind of poetry I am acquainted with. The new forms of poetry seem to change the way I think, and in a way they have been turning me into poetry, I do believe. I've been reading other poems too, old slim books that folks left round Innisfree. Thinking a poem is like the first trip to Byzantium all over again, it feels like that each time. The more Artsy Boy shows me new poems, the more my everyday notions slip into the rushing river, collective like, of words.

Stand up on a rotting log amidst the thousands of stalks—tuber gone astral, lit fish in cosmic stream, faces of some gone family overrun with water—up on log to better see above the greens, which is a take-off strip out of boughs to the forked fate paths. Elkhead. There in the glitter of baby greens I witness the swimming elk, doing the shoulder crawl through the leaves under the scorched icicle rays of the sun. Running from me or just playing, sometimes I can't tell. This corner of the ranch is where wild ones leap in and over and out and through and mix 'n mate with the farmed ones, or so I have suspected all along because of the unusually aggressive and skittish behaviour of certain stock.

When elk present straight on crag, set against the milky way, the ancient bugle contains a rosehip sauciness and high-pitched purple moosiness. When the domestic dog howls, it does so through the mime of wolf lips. Elkhead is contained in that bugle just like Wolfhead is in the howl. When it bugles that music, it summons up their ancestors, the giant elk, who are in fact metallic sculptures made of myth—specimens from Memily's yard art.

A great shot, like a visual epic. I want to film these shots leading up to the canoe scenes, Inkster. A slow shot of the elk disappearing.

You better not be making the movie for what's his name.

For who?

For Ma—Ma—Ma—Ma . . .

No, not for.

Where are you, Samson?

●

Cut. Clear. Cutted Cutter Curt Cult Corpse Clean. Cleave.
Erosion on the banks of history cutback cutup cutlery cut-
throat. Clear sky, clear my hands. One finger a leaf; one
finger a pine cone; one finger to touch the cold fluid on
this branch; one finger to touch the edge of the wound.
Screaming weakness.

o

Danger. Danger in the air. I was in the outhouse and saw danger through a knot hole in the door that a cylinder of sunlight pokes through. A Hyperion galloped over the grass. Closer and closer until I closed my eyes, because it was about to ram the outhouse. But nothing substantial hit me. It felt like something passed through me on its way to somewhere else.

And, you know, Cheryl came over to me and said I was on all fours, just about ten paces in front of the outhouse. I was on my knees and also my elbows, and holding two tike paddles that usually hang in the outhouse to my temples and waving them slowly around apparently saying, antlers, antlers!

I guess I am just like you, Cheryl. We are both marginal. Like the elks are. I have become irrelevant to the projects of Innisfree. The new generation is virtual, and I am stuck in the entrails.

Then zhe told me I was what zhe called genrequeer. And I had to agree with her. That's right—at some point I stopped measuring myself against the men out here, I started modelling myself after the dames instead.

●

Heli-drone blades make pudding of air above hemlock, stark water dripping off canopy, water falling to weakness, numbness, trembling. Whirlpool. Fall into crotch of Western Maple. On back, surrounded by Sword Ferns and Black-eyed Susans. Up there, the search unit hovering. Down here, huge drops of dew. A grasshopper sipping at spherical spring. Moss pieces clinging to charred arm stump. Plush petals of moist flower sun juices through straws through mouths of watery light gasping. Up there. Then strength shoots again. Curl up like toothpaste. But upward and onward said grandmother, ov'r feather moss, terrace of rock, through a stream, becomes a creek; dunk noggin, splash, drink. Seared skin comes off in water, floating heel flaps.

o

Life is getting too complicated for the Enderbee we love and the Innisfree that we know, and it's giving me headaches. I shall leave everything to the ranch hands for the day and return to the beginning, which isn't too much to leave or too far to go, for elk and ranch hands look after themselves pretty good, and the beginning is only on the other edge of Byzantium. I take the paths that mukluks first stomped down, feeling that closeness through those footfalls to the tradition of animal and the bond of the rib. Changes my view of Byzantium coming in from the other direction to the highway by the new prison, the way I first came here with the cattle trailer full of my elks, how many years ago. Through that village archway, "The gateway to the supreme north," so it states. The statue of the chief and of the rainbow salmon and of the train, also of the barn with the black scars from fire and age: all of it still there in sideways pour of four o'clock sunlight. And farther over, that is the hotel—the white one with the tall sign and the tropical-themed rooms, done up with real palms and waterslide—I stayed in when I first arrived at Byzantium. Recall how I parked the elk trailer there beside the gas pump and horse posts. Had the four-legged troop on sedatives to keep them from going reindeer on me, painful-hoofed they were from the journey up from Squashington. Ah yes, what memories they are.

Neon contours of jukebox glass case. Finger stains above choices. The international city robbed me of any personality. Why I was on the move? I mean to the country. Remember.

Going down into this old pioneer bar that is now boarded up . . . the person inside who was doing the performance, the one who took the whole town under his downy wing and had us do and say those things.

Snapped his fingers, made those sounds, said deeper and deeper into blissful relaxation you are falling. The velvet antlers in the shape of humans are falling towards the earth. Left margin to right margin right margin to left margin.

o

I imagined something in a daydream, or maybe I saw it. Cheryl was there in a tree house, perched in vanilla-coloured pumps with each foot on a different board hammered to the tree, boards torn from the collapsing wall of an old forest shack falling over in a slow wave of natural demolition. Cheryl's skirt looked at first like a tattered flag. What are you doing staring in the moon mirror, Cheryl? I am staring at you, behind me, zhe said. There is a great threat.

Like a catastrophe?

Yes, said Memily. Now it is Memily on this trail.

Under the rocks, in the rocks. In the rocks are what is coming, said Cheryl again.

A really, really, really powerful one. A powerful charge, said Mars Ares, suddenly back on the scene in a poof of pink phosphorus. Where do you think all the aggregate goes? It goes up the mountain's nose, said Mars.

Samson! I thought. Samson, Samson is out there, Samson is waxing his mustache, Samson is trimming his pubic hair, Samson, Samson is covered in coal dust or something. At the back of the closet, in the inner room. I cannot go any farther.

Mars Ares and Inkster are doing lines of the elk powder and they are turning into god-powerful creatures, said Dan-the-Man, coming out from behind one of the I's.

o

It was on that journey that the exhaust from one of the bitumenlite compressor stations kept blowing in my face and giving me unnatural daydreams. That is when the horrific revelation of Mars Ares' plan became apparent, and the nasty connection with me who was the unwanting person who just stumbled upon his plan.

I came across Mars Ares inside the Other Barn. Had his sleeves rolled up and was building something in the back.

That elk was no typical elk; there was something not normal in its stride. Like a mechanical animal at a fairground exhibit in the futuristic fall fairs they have in Byzantium these days.

I stood gandering at him for what felt like a longer time than I reckon it actually was. So skinny without his cloak on, without his janitor's sweatshirt, without his tall hat, and then he started to look like a featherless owl or something, did Mars Ares, who had placed a headset on one of the antlerless Hyperion which flashed lights in the corners of its bulgy eyes timed according to some sort of complicated sequence, to make it dart and run in a certain direction as if spooked by headlights that were causing shadows in a willow swale.

Now Mars, I said. Let's be kind, now. Times have changed . . .

Mars Ares pulled cylinders from a metal box that had vapour puffing out the cracks, then tied a whole bunch of cylinders to the elk's underside.

Inkster. Come here. Hold the head straight, he said.

Though he was an intruder in my barn, there was sense to what he said. He's made a tunnel into its third stomach into which something would be stored.

No. Yes. No. Yes. Mars? What are you doing in this cave?

Then he showed me a series of diagrams of the elk dodging left and right according to the directions from the blinkers, then exploding like firing circuitry once it gets up to a ridge.

●

Muffled clunk duffled weaponry. Moon zooming. Gasbro militia hunting the goat. Hold so still, lamb, until the lion's gaze falls into the bee-ringing flowers. Baby deer in the innocent shadows. Jaws, lantern eyes, wanging pain in disappeared arm. Skies are parting to deserted shore. Galilee, Galilee, name without substance. Orlando, Orlando. Westminster. Where the final chime strikes the rocks the river shall open. I, my. My I. Ants do six-step dance on the side of my belly, spiders crouch on my warmth, a coyote snout sniffing through the bush, cold mucus in my lobed satellite. Preaches twisted colon we came from worms. Pull fob from front pouch of overalls. Thumb elk fob. Feel it vibrate with each relay of timed ping. Fire elk is on his way. This nook in the trees eases the pain. Staring. Need to keep warm. The warmth of the sun making mist on the greens. With one good arm tender the limbs of a balsam. Chew bark. Sense carcass nearby. Smells of lice and museums, hair and dust, closet and buffalo. One hand at side, roll over on good side, get up. Press the contact lichen to let the Bone Healer know you are coming.

●

Whispering the word bomb twice. Feeling the collateral damage of that final silent letter pronounced with aplomb. Second b after m. A sphere with a wick. Make a statement. Set an example. Systematic. Forward. Onward. Through. Each moment attaches to the next in a chain. Every day to day season to each season life to life. Until rupture. Non-arm phases from numbness to fire to pain again. To pain. Cain. Pain is a ruby guider. Hider. Brother town. Not enough moss blanket to pull around. Reaching monkey hands into the wrenches. Swinging from the gears of the stars with monkey wrench arms. The sound of the bird induces. The sound of the plane overhead, and of the helicopter. Left margin to right margin right margin to left margin.

Asleep in a cavity of loam poetry.

o

Even though everything's in disarray with media and law, the July 1 parade must go on. On old farm machines, the people of Byzantium and the district of Enderbee are represented in the streets on floats. They go past the huge statue of the fisher people and the lumberjacks. The mountains in the background are picture-postcard perfect. The bomber has been silent for months, and the town has moved on to cheerier agendas. Of course Samson Huckleberry's in the parade, doing his organic-egg juggling act, on a unicycle no less. Each egg painted a different colour, he's looping these eggs, cross-eyed from concentrating so hard, eggs which are supposed to represent the different points of view of the entire universe. His small, acrobatic body can flip through time. He leaves the parade early to go pick up more eggs after a couple fumbles.

Then there's the Carlyles, the ragtag bunch of them. They're all blasting locally famous folk-metal songs from built-in sound systems. Scooting around the parade floats on Mommy race car and Daddy hummer, dirt bike Son and Daughter big rig.

And here is Cheryl Hill dressed in a bear outfit next to former Mayor Timothy, together waving the Byzantium flag, knocking hips, on the turret of a huge mining machine which straddles the entire street, so the odd onlooker has to step back into a doorway and dip around the sides of a store. Their banner says: "Byzantium-Always-Byzantium."

Dan-the-Man and Memily are portaging their Canoe of Complicity over their heads like Mr. and Mrs. Canoe Head, or something, wearing the solemn smiles of art popes. Heading somewhere with that signature canoe to launch into the water, following the parade down Yeats St.

Then there was me upcountry, taking a looksee at all this through a telescope I formed by partly closing each fist so there's a hole, and then lining up my fists and peering through.

The parade day, when there are items to be dealt with around the ranch, and matches or lighter to be found. Time to raise the floorboards and do the job for the community.

Had the duffle bag clutched in my hand, I did, and there was a young man's vigour apparent in my step as I stole away with it. Bohemian waxwings and nothern flickers and Stellar's jays in the leafy chinks of the tree-wall along the sides of the Scylla road that continued down there. What else could I call that place than "down there," down, down into the valley where the roaring pits of humanity resound.

My summer hat tipped in the attitude of the mountain slope while elk leapt back and forth, arrow-kneed blur in and out of the fenceline and the treeline, transparent-like exchange of full stealthy bodies.

I'd pried open the floorboards at Innisfree farmhouse and removed a bag, I had, noticing there was only one, labelled Head Expander, one that weighed more than a sack of potatoes. Were there supposed to be two bags? And why was I doing this? Left margin to right margin.

Looked off the cliff again. Always a parade, like the charade in any great unfolding. The Innisfree group thought I should be at the parade. Aw, Inkster, we will miss ya. Come down soon as you're done.

'Kay, I'd said.

So now here I am, waiting for nightfall. Can see Artsy Boy doing his thing. Dressed like a charlatan of flames, some combination of historical warrior and old continental god of some sort, always one for the unusual, he is, but I'm not sure people will really understand his vision and how he shows it off.

And well, hell, har har, look at that, there's John, the pipe carrier, and his cousin who owns the car wash. Both of them getting a chuckle out of Samson, as he's juggling and unicycling too.

Adjust the focus on my hand telescope by loosening and tensing some finger muscles to better follow the Innisfree procession. Yes, good advertising it is for the tours, look at them all on the wagon, sitting and standing on hay blocks wearing pioneer clothes. Those ranch hands done well this year, helped out by some kids running along with the mechanical elk by the reins, which is just a real elk fitted with some armour that was fashioned into elk molds courtesy of one of the ranch hands who also happens to be a hobby smith.

Then a scuffle of some folks starts to break out. The mechanical elk tears away from the float procession and starts going bonkers, knocking someone off balance—Mrs. Primrose, by the looks of it—strutting awkwardly into the hills that turn into mountains, chased by one of the ranch hands, the tough lass with the sense of humour.

But I don't have time to see the end of that situation, because I hear the song sparrow unsheathe its song from its throat and I know, it's time for the difficult show in the gloaming. Yes, everything is descending at a good clip, this place so wide it shoots fibres of joy through the many acreages of the heart.

Now I pull out the black tubes from the duffle bag, taped together with a smooth electric wrap, jab them one by one into the sand, also wedging some into the fracture lines of rocks on the cliff edge.

Pull out the remote from the side pocket of the duffle bag, and, after driving a safe distance up the road, get out, clear my throat, and hit the red sensor. Gosh, how does this thing work again? Thumb press, thumb press, thumb press.

From down below, they will see the mighty bright explosion from the cliff, and the big word shot over the many other shapes and colours already afloat. In magnesium letters, it will say OIL AND GAS FOR UTOPIA, kablamo.

That's me, the fireworks guy. Side-gig type of thing, you see. Elk tours can only take you so far.

OIL AND GAS FOR UTOPIA drifts down and dissipates in vapour scraps over the parade. An important phrase that the new mayor wanted to have said in the fireworks.

Byzantiumites are cheering, appreciating the mighty fine show, if I do say so myself. They just keep getting better year to year, they do.

And Mars Ares, an organic farmer new to town and the donator of the fireworks, who is going to employ hundreds in the new zucchini and cucumber greenhouses that are in turn afforded by the donations from the oil and gas industry, or at least according to the new mayor, he gives me the thumbs up, I can see that through my hand telescope, I think.

But after letting off the fireworks and driving the rest of the way down to pick up some of the ranch hands and go back to Innisfree, that's when we know something more than just fireworks has occurred, because there are fires on the other ridge, over on the Charybdis side. A feel in the air, the one a farmer gets when they know the worst thing is occurring, by seasonal forces uncontrollable—to crops, to family, to a way of life.

I know it because I can smell something coming, like a poisonous ozone before an unnatural storm. The black wave in the sky.

A huge bird made of blackest humours, with a burning fringe of fire and smoke. It blazes inward from the edges and plunges into the valley in a plumed waterfall of darkness and moon-sized crackles and tar-pail aromas confusing and deadening to the nose.

Bombs Are Not Metaphors: Sam Sears

—1 July 2038—

The environmental mass collective Anti-Everything is decrying Gasbro's business-as-usual plan to continue construction of Pipe Nexus 3, saying the 2030 Workers Safety Act guarantees paid leave in extraordinary threat scenarios.

Increasing the anti-Pipe Nexus 3 heat are public figures speaking up for the bombers in solidarity.

"The bombings speak for the 85 per cent of western Can'tadians unwilling to accept another large industrial project in some of the last remaining pristine rainforest and salmon rivers of the planet. The 'One Ecosystem' theory introduced by McDavid Zucchini Junior speaks to the cumulative benefit that large untouched wild zones contribute to the global biosphere."

Gravy to Overthrow the Cheese Curds has claimed mock responsibility for last year's bombings, posting that they are proud to have put an end to Gasbro production, if but for one day.

GOCC is notorious for falsely admitting to crimes. When asked why they chose a humorous name for their dead-serious platform, and why they make public fools of themselves, the representative of GOCC stated they just want to show off "an example *par excellence*" of what they call "Come On! You! Nism." Their mandate and political platform is in fact to alter, very seriously, the substance of Can'tada through belly laughter, yuk yuk yoga, Guitar Hero therapy, and '40s dress-up mountain climbing tours. *Gravy to Overthrow the Cheese Curds* also aims to "attempt putting 'an end to the end' of the age of irony."

Interim mayor of Byzantium, Sam Sears, is quoted by GOCC today as crying out: "These bombings are not some kind of metaphor!" Which, as the writers of the 'end to the end' of irony note, was an ironic statement considering the prose-poem feed that is unravelling through the *Troutsource* portal decoder.

Troutsource is one of the only news blogs with a staff capable of tracking the movers and shakers within the increasingly virtual and confusing world. Like us, baby. Like us and support us using the pay feature at the top.

Gravy to Overthrow Cheese Curds link:

Listen, Peter Menbridge, as we all know, the gunk tar sands are very much an economically essential cesspool. That is why our party has taken upon itself to show all citizens the sanitary measures necessary to keep the idea of our nation clean. Look, Peter, there will always be people who are going to oppose these large projects, which admittedly have significant impacts on the environment. This government, though, Peter, is doing everything in its power, Peter, to reduce these impacts, Peter, and ensure industry can benefit all Can'tadians, Peter. Recent socialist media postings of the Minister of Defense shaking hands with a rapist-murderer Commander-Sergeant from the Can'tadian Air Force is bad media practice. So is focusing on our tendency to joke about sadomasochism in public address. Peter, that you, a DED veteran, are still alive to witness my Parlepasliament's record-length term in office, is a testament to I don't know what, maybe cryogenics. Sure, you may still smell the reek coming in through the crack around the door. We may, every one of us in this room, be aware of the same overflowing toilet down the hall that has persisted for decades. But rest assured that my party provides the best smell retardants to cover up the stench and plunge the superpower movement forward, to see that this necessary cesspool rises, Peter M, you Che Guevara of liberal news. You love a good barbecue with your family on the lake. You must,

Peter, adore being surrounded by the grasses, the mountains, the birds, while you scrub the grill for another batch of shish kabobs. These natural beauties sustain a certain kind of wealth, Peter, no doubt about it. Think of it as wealth B, the God-given endowment. Now look up from the grass and dragonflies, notice the computers and the cars. This is also a kind of wealth, Peter, call it wealth A, human wealth. It's the money we generate from wealth A that provides us with the ability to sustain wealth B. Without the large screen TVs, we would have no beaver sanctuary, Peter. Let us not forget the human. The amount of tax revenue generated by the oil sands is nothing less than extensively Homo sapiens. Look, Peter, we don't have the benefit of celebrities on our side pushing our cause like the environmentalist lobby. Biased media like Troutsource, funded as they are by environmental multinationals, should be read with a huge grain of salt. Listen, Peter, we know you like handcuffs . . . Listen, Peter, here, I'll bend over for you, now stick your nose in my bum and inhale. Clean like I told you, eh?

o

We'd retreated to Innisfree in a hurry, hoping that the feeling of dread would stay back there in town. I was watching the prose poem stream in the kitchen on Dan's screen, while I prepared feed bottles for one of the calves whose mother had been taken by the disease. A ranch hand came into the kitchen while I was doing that, and saw me gandering at the screen and she laughed.

You look confused, Inkster.

I don't get it, I said. Seems to me that all the poems they're showing, all the bombing and such, none of that's really happened, you know, in real life, otherwise I would hear and see an explosion just happen, don't you think?

Just keep watching, said the ranch hand. She came over and grabbed a couple of the nursing bottles from me to take back for the calf that was in the healing manger.

It's happening in the future, she said. None of this has happened yet, and maybe it won't ever happen. But it's sure a pretty neat bit of work, that website is.

Yes, I said. Yes, er . . . Well, I am going to watch some more poetry, I will, and then I will come out and help nurse Dolly with you guys.

All right. Looks kind of crazy on that screen. Almost as crazy as your firework show. A little smoky, wasn't it!

Um, yeah.

You know what, Inkster?

What?

You should try reading the poems out loud. You might find they are realer that way.

Wrist of good arm bubbling. What? A melted band. What? From the parade. For participants. Melted onto skin. Parade. Charade. Doe's eyes poke between bush blades, massive-eyed concern. Awake again. Whatever it was passed onward. Sick animal bedded down for final nap under funereal leafage. Doe licking my forehead. Indicating to me I must get up. They are coming this way. Four-legged friends arrive with a way forward. What end. The hooves. A hoofed friend. A hoofed friend's lick wakens me again. The armoured god of the place between wood and field still in one piece attaboy. Motor sound out of truck context. Down side of cliff, another animal path, but slip. Stuck in clump of krummholz on ledge that's singing a northern melody across the lips of a cold flute. Enderbee landscape visible in valley.

Bone Healer, will you help me
If your problem is bone-related
My cartilage aches
Then you must eat catfish
And you have some
Yes, here, eat this catfish
Thank you
Dashed with some salt of the elk's brow
Thank you
It has been cooking for you for centuries
Thank you.

You mind-swapped.
Really?
It happens
How?
Though poetry
Sounds bad
It can get you into trouble
I am in trouble
Yes you are

Will you tell me who done it?
You mean who you are?
I guess so.

Insidious insights. Bone Healer grabs my hand and bites and bites and bites these patterns onto my skin. Smoke and steam. See everything about her that is him and it and we she feeds me the him the it the we drink. Why must any story be an ordeal? Ideal ordeal. My face hangs in an animal grin, a forward concentration, my jaw and tongue so heavy. A one-armed journey

Through the muskeg
Through the swamp
Around the lake
Between two rivers
Over a mountain pass

You oiled the entire town, bravo. Someone lit a smoke and the whole town went up. You caused Armageddon on a miniature scale. How do you feel about that? It's a Pompeii down there.

○

Just a cavern with diagonal rock walls, and ashes from a campfire, it is obvious that the Bone Healer was helping heal the bomber who is dying from shock—to even reverse what happened.

The sun, the moon, the day and night, the repetition of left margin to right margin has brought us through the shadows and the light to the place where the Bone Healer resides. This is where the person had crawled.

I followed him on *PodView*.

Wow, I said. I looked at the stream of words and pictures and sounds, as they sped along the *PodView* and got materialized through the bit-decoder into some sort of fuzzy picture of someone crawling within a scrambled portion of darkness.

What do you make of it, Inkster? Asked the ranch hand after I left for the healing manger to help feed.

It doesn't make much sense to me.

Like the little pieces of everybody's world?

No, not quite like that at all.

Pipe Nexus Called Worst Disaster Since Sea Swell

—4 July 2038—

The oil spill in Byzantium of three days ago caused by a massive rupture of a bitumenlite arterial in Pipe Nexus 3 will stand as the defining image of disaster of the 2030s, Andrew Coppernickle opined in a morning blog post.

Coppernickle's book, *X Marks the Drop* (2027), surveyed pivotal mega calamities through time. On top of the North Polar Frost Heave of the 1960s, the Chernobyl disaster in the 1980s, the Rwanda genocide in the 1990s, 9/11 in the 2000s, the Bread Basket Bust of the 2010s, the Mass Sea Swell of the 2020s, Coppernickle has added what he calls the Black Vesuvius Rupture of 2038.

The disaster is unfathomable in its sadness (see the *Troutstream* link at the bottom for images), with hundreds of Byzantiumites possibly suffocated in condensed petroleum products or burned alive. The Can'tadian government has invoked the War Measures Act for the first time since the FLQ crisis.

Experts say the cleanup of this 10 million barrel spill is all but impossible, and Gasbro executive Chase Beefrude is advising that the Disaster Board condemn the valley.

"The thickness of the spill makes the cleaning task profoundly difficult," said Tex Mason of the Cleanup Board.

CEO Beefrude was unavailable for comment, and reports from The Enderbee Endtimes has him quoted previously stating that high-pressure pipeline technology will be "reevaluated" in the coming weeks and months, and that "Pipe Nexus 3 was designed to be bomb-proof."

The mobbing of the engineer who designed the pipe is underway, as people have oil-balled his home in USmonton already (see *PodView*).

●

Who knows what is happening out there beyond cave.
Hope they are okay. Hope this was all a joke. Now the
Bone Healer is pushing the fiery fist of Mars Ares back into
the fissure. Stealing the hypnosis back again, now doing
it in reverse.

(a single bleating of the elk)
(language telluric)

every word is bomb
said is exploding
every word is a bomb
together damaging
ten tintinnabulations
said together
five tintinnabombulations
said together
detonating together

Apple Pie and
Cream Soda—
say
hello
and so does
Butter
(from under the Lid)

After bedtime snack, bedded, a big book open on chest
the weight on ribs makes breathing fatiguing
reading the words makes lids heavy
eyes follow the words, eye sewn to margin

from left margin to right margin, right margin
to left margin, left margin to right margin, right margin
to left margin, left margin to right margin, right margin
to left margin, and so on, and so on, eye sewn to margin

THAT HURT DIDN'T IT. THAT HURT THAT HURT THAT

IT HURT IT URTS IT RTS IT UR IT URT IT URTS IT U IT IS T U
IT I TI I IT IT IT IT IT IT IT IT IS I I I I

    Now let go of the arm of Ares, and grab the wing
    of the reaching owl

right margin to left margin, left margin
to right margin, right margin to left margin, left margin
to right margin, right margin to left margin, left margin
to left margin to left margin

Move now? Yes, can move now. Back outside tunnel,
looking down towards Byzantium. Slippy slide of black oil
down hill tumbling into Byzantium. Only coldness from
arm stump. Out of the cave of the Bone Healer. Congealed

tar up to knees. Slimy viscosity. Pain gone. Memory back. Cannot believe. I have no ID, I don't exist. Should have listened to Inkster, warning of Mars Ares with his pendulum. Like Darth Vader, or the Evil Circus Leader from the show Dustbowl, the Kurtz character or George's boss, the anthropomorphism of the unknown. A nature which tempts us to self-destruct. It's the same person in all the minds of the writers, the invisible character of plot, right Inkster?

o

Even the old-fashioned television footage Dan-the-Man was playing for us, it was too broken up to see proper; there were lines and all kinds of distortions moving through it.

Dan grabbed the television and shook it back and forth to try to get better reception.

That's the problem when you try to run a digital source back through an analog decoder, Dan cursed.

It's too late to save them, but what about us, is Enderbee okay? asked Dan-the-Man, sounding uncertain as we stared at the multicoloured distortion with mouths gaping.

I guess, we are a good 30 kilometres from town. Innisfree will go unharmed, I reckoned. But hopefully there isn't another explosion . . . and people can get out of town.

We were hugging each other, squeezing tears into a communal bucket.

Everything out the window swam through the teary lens, the growing smudge.

Inkster? Memily rubbed my back.

He always loved you, I said, out of the blue.

What?

Dan-the-Man tried to shield Memily with his big arm from what he thought might be emotional violence of a kind.

I always hated how you shielded me, Dan, said Memily. Like a goat-skin condom.

Have you thought of Squashington, I said? You and

Samson could . . .

Look! Dan was pointing.

A huge plume of smoke was rising from where Byzantium would be in the distance.

We need to muster everyone together, said Memily.

Where is Cheryl? We need to get Cheryl.

But first we scream, first we must scream. Dan inhaled really, really, really deep as if he could blow, blow, blow the smoke far, far away into outer space.

Death flames floating on the oil slick as tea lights. Fall and roll and paddle sludge hill single arm resisting the spin of body. Cellphone store hit hard by deluge. Handheld gadgets little surfboards floating desks people staggering through streets in robes of goopy petroleum. Off City Hall fascia hang columns of condensed oil stiffened into stalactites. And many of those who'd been participating in outdoor activities glued to the streets. Arms and legs sticking out and necks too as though emerging from thick coffee. Hockey stick made of rigid bitumenlite. Many-limbed bitumen soak pile next to an overturned float like turtle. The ex-Mayor Timothy bitumenlite statue of congress of someone crawling in the direction of Gasbro headquarters. Expression recalls Terry Fox in final stretch. One arm down. One up. Stiffened into some sort of patriotic salute. Eyes flush with tears of gas. A pharaoh of some small land. He who had moved around town, so omnipresent, he who had shaken all the townsfolk's hands by the hot dog stand, whose speeches by the podium pandered to the taxpayer and the evader, who had repeated the same speeches at different events, but who remembered everyone's nickname. Emergency trucks. Cross. Red Cross. Whole Northwest on a cross. Sick forest. Sickness in the stressed tree system. Empty forests after black magic beetles. Stumble. But this is it. The turning point. The tipping point. A blackened bronze sheen covering all. The rescue team, webbed people pulling me from oil onto a stretcher. Wiping me down with huge rags that smell like paint thinner. A truck trailer full of the towns-folk, flopping around like pelicans, to higher safe zone. The medics figure my arm was blown off in the explosions here in town. Tumult of the myths seems over. Nothing but the oil-soaked aftermath. Taking me away. Someone always taken away. On a truck over to the hospital some-where. Everything. Nothing. Everything. Never access this valley or the ranch again. Slabbed over thing.

o

Heck no, I don't eat fried chicken no more. Even though all the country songs say I do.

See, I knew a neighbour who had fried chicken almost daily. Keeled over from a heart attack at age fifty.

When I was a little boy, I went out to the middle of a ball field and I began spinning with my arms cocked like chicken wings, and looking up into the great feathery sky and felt the wings of the mind. And then things got dizzy, and in a blur I ended up here in these fields to the north.

That's the wind that got me here.

I walked out into the perfect stillness of my bean rows knowing I am a custodian of something wonderful.

Then two helicopters descended.

They are here to keep cleaning up the far corner of the ranch where the memories of Brandy and the kids inhaling the fumes from the crude oil are.

I inhaled the fumes and it had no particular effect upon me.

How did the chicken cross the road outside of Kentucky Fried Chicken?

In a box!

See, I still have a joke or two up my sleeve.

o

The last time I spoke to Samson, he was ripping up his final love letter to Memily and talking funny about stuff.

Once you free your elk, you will be a hero, Inkster. Left margin to right margin.

Free my elk? Left margin to right margin. I have no idea what happened to you, Samson. Right margin to left margin. And you know the coyotes and wolves would get them if I let them go just like that.

Never mind, Inkster. Up until now, you've been a quite weak character in the story of one of the protesters, right margin. A kind of sitter-on-the-fence type of guy, left margin, but by setting your elk free, right margin, by doing the big thing, left margin, you become an active character, right margin to left margin.

Oh?

Yes. Like me, I am doing a video pamphlet. A video to help protect one of the rivers. To protect Lethe . . . from light pollution.

Oh?

Yes sir, each egg is a perspective. Each egg painted a different colour, a cascade between my blurred palms, each egg a speckled bomb opening up a point of view from the land hand.

Samson and I had hiked to the back of Innisfree as he practiced juggle-walking for the upcoming parade, and then we got to work cutting open the fence.

What's that duffle bag you got there, Inkster? Left margin to right margin.

Bone Healer gave it to me. Right margin to left margin.
Bone Healer? You mean Skull Crusher!
Here, follow me through the columbines.
Okay, but you take the bag, said Samson.
No, you take it, I said.
No, you take it. I already have my bag.
(Twittering of a thrush.)

Idyllic Ranch Breeding Ground for Terror

—21 August 2038—

An elk farmer named Jeffery Inkster has been charged with causing what some have called the worst ecological catastrophe in the history of PC Columbia and Cowberta. The mounties surrounded his tourist elk farm, making several arrests.

"Like many who live the idealist life, there was another story to him," the former mayor, Timothy Pleaser, was recorded as saying, mere days before he was critically injured.

"It doesn't surprise me that Jeffery packed explosives," the ex-mayor had said.

The exact role Inkster played in the bomb plot is still unclear. However, police say a search of his ranch turned up a duffle bag which sampled positive for plastic explosive residue.

This was combined into a garage operation using clock parts and a series of lithium proton batteries contained in a patchwork of various stolen industrial explosives.

Manifestoes, poems, and other items related to an art sabotage plot were seized from huts and yurts occupied by squatters in Innisfree. Some of this radicalized group volunteered on Inkster's elk ranch, and he is thought to have acted as their figurehead.

Line searches are underway through other properties of Enderbee for the vanished elk farmer. The search team encountered not a single elk on the property. The reason for their disappearance was explained by a 50-metre tear in the fence, say searchers.

o

I looked for the boy, I did, for I feared he'd wandered astray, and could be out there in the mountains, hoping, through suicide, to join the elk on their retreat between the eskers and into the alpine pass. I reckon activists and filmmakers like Samson believed they needed to come work on a ranch such as mine to relearn forgotten skills and smell the tang of fur. Then they discovered the contradiction of farming and turned against me with a whole bunch of isms. One day they turned against Innisfree, they did, taking several Mnemosyne and Hyperions hostage. Me and Samson responded, like mature people do to smart criticism, and we adapted. Okay, okay, I'll stop doing the velvet antler, I promised. I'll just sell their adrenaline glands instead and make ashtrays out of their hoofs. The people who came to Innisfree were disappointed to see there is nothing here, not even a real role model. We let the elk go, actually. Sorry.

But that—and by *that* I mean all you have seen on this tour of Innisfree—happened before you could see the outlines of my thoughts when you looked into the land. That's what one of my ranch hands told me on the last day of Innisfree. Claimed he saw my inner eye in the cloud 'bove the valley. Inkster Intelligence of some sort, gone into the land.

Medieval is what she called it, the one who said my thoughts had been ground up with earth and bound together with the minerals. Said that was the way it had always been before a certain time, when spirit and matter were together. River to ranch, stream to fence, forest to plain, evergreen to broadleaf. Bowing my head to the giving earth, like a sunflower looking down on what it grows out of . . .

Everybody out there was living the lives of tokens, folks in a board game of identity. All the faces in the town, the face of the artist and the face of the mayor, the fire fighter's moccasin head, they could all fit snug in a deck of cards, shuffled and stacked and laid face down, to be pulled at random and analyzed.

The hunters desire racks too, they sure do. The elk were my servants as much as I was theirs. Antlers slave to our worship.

To head out there when the moon is on a star-chain and it has become the stationary pendulum. It's like living in an exploded story welded back together, smooth and lean, lean like elk meat.

(The meat of the elk is sheathed in fat, unlike the fat in beef, which beads.)

Elk Farmer Unfazed by Arrest

—14 October 2038—

Several witnesses report that when law enforcement showed up yesterday at Innisfree Ranch they found elk farmer Inkster stumbling in circles at the centre of a field playing a boxed musical instrument called the hurdy-gurdy, singing a love song, apparently unrequited.

Elk farmer Jeffery Inkster, charged with eleven counts of capital crime, claims that a hypnotist was responsible for coercing people of Enderbee into participating in the bomb plot.

Today at a Cancougar court Inkster claimed that a man with "white mustache and white sweatshirt," who was trained in a powerful combination of Eye Movement Desensitization Reprogramming, hypnagogic inducement, and post-hypnotic cueing, had sent several townspeople into a destructive swoon.

"Mars Ares had a trained thrush. Had animal pictures clipped from rustic magazines," Inkster testified.

The hypnosis theory will be inadmissible at Inkster's trial, say lawyers, as it has never been proven that this technique can achieve a totalizing takeover of an individual's will. Doctor Sigmund Skinner took the stand to testify that hypnotic techniques have no visible effect on heart rate, body temperature, or central cognitive patterns, making it highly unlikely that such techniques could ever be used to manipulate people into performing extremist acts.

Further threatening Inkster's case is the media climate *Troutsource* has noted before: news centres are no fans of ambiguity. They need their bad guy, and it doesn't matter if the person is innocent or guilty, so long as they fit the description of a bearded angry person (aside from during the Stanley Cup playoffs).

Once the guru-like elk farmer, Jeffery Inkster—the same man who sawed off and made powder from the antlers of his beloved farm animals—is now disgraced.

Inkster is unrepentant about his complicity in the plot, and seems not to regret the tragic events surrounding his bizarre operation: "The ranch was a stepping stone to a new life, and a new place, and it doesn't matter where I am, I am forever in that place. Now I am free to go to jail, because the past has gone home. Memily, Cheryl Hill, Samson, even the Carlyles, are free to live in the real future now, in the real Enderbee, in the real world after the spill, after the antlers, and after Innisfree."

●

Sometimes it is a mega ranch, other times an oil site. They call it the urban forest where tree clones are planted by the unknowing for the unknown. Silvery pipes annex the earth, connecting with other pipelines that network through aspen systems suckering and sprouting downwind from sulphur emissions. The rain crashes from nimbus Olympus onto the amphibian breast to sacrifice. Above the mouse burrows and the rusted pitchfork stuck in the stump, within this nowhere grove filled with many things, a circle of cloaked figures reciting fibrous verse in a language drawn from the earth. Mermaid worms you swim the silky soils, Class-6 drainages, absorbing this escaping. Writhe slimy tails in the wet pebbles along riparian passage.

○ ●

Jeffery Inkster would have been searching for me that night after the fireworks and into the next day. I know he would have been checking for me along the base of Charybdis Ridge. Then, not finding me, walking back to Innisfree through the gap we had torn in the fence. From there, he would have seen the ridge erupt in a black gulf. I think he would have been on the verge of cardiac arrest. He would suddenly remember. Everything. Me. The second duffle bag. Mars Ares. How the Bone Healer sent Mars Ares back into history with a counter-hypnosis that also got Skull Crusher banished.

I imagine Inkster searching for me behind the fence. Hands lost in overall pockets for soul change as he stumbles after me. Remembering how a few weeks before, I had left the parade early after whiffing uncharacteristically on the juggle cascade, beginning to suspect. Then forgetting on cue. Then digging in his pocket with his whole arm to pull out his ancient oh so ancient wallet, to look at a head-and-shoulders shot of Mnemosyne. "Mnemosyne, oh Mnemosyne . . . Titan of all animals," he would sigh.

Innisfree was Inkster's art. But its closure was his masterpiece. I bet every so often he still scratches his head and wonders if it actually was me who did the deed. It was indeed, I cry out, from my new humble life as an amputee, in a wet, readerly city somewhere on the coast of Squashington. It was me, and by extension it was you, Inkster, for we were both antlers of the same Elkhead. Now that I had footage of everything that transpired, you must have known what I was going to do with it.

I imagine Inkster saying, "The elk are on the move through the vertical forests of time, they smell the odour of freedom in their fellow's arse, which propels them over the pass into the mountains beyond the eskers, past Lethe and into the open." He is saying, "I wish I could play my gurdy under the fulsome sky, that they come galloping back over the grass and stones to show me the way into the open, but the elks don't listen to that song anymore. They are fled from the chorus of country tunes."

That is what Inkster said, though it is my lips now which whisper these words as I sit drinking a soy latte in Portlandsea. I was the director all along. The one who can dress up as anything. As Ares, the God of War.

Derrida Bloom's Afterword

Stacked on top of zoological themes, this book also name-drops from Greek mythology as well as Canadian mythology, both Indigenous and Settler. The bull elk are called Hyperion after the creator of the sun and moon, while the elk cows are named Mnemosyne, who was the god of memory and mother of the muses. Both Hyperion and Mnemosyne were born from Gaia, the earth, and presumably the supreme elk mama.

The river of forgetfulness, Lethe, flows through this story. Gods of war and rage, Ares and Mars, share characteristics and become one nebulous figure. Ares represents the destructive power of rage, while Mars brings the side of agriculture and peacekeeping to the noise impulse. Poised in the background is the industrial magistrate Zeus, as well as Persephone, goddess of, for the purpose of this story, the mining underworld.

The same politics that saw the titan gods get supplanted by the Olympians in mythical history seem to be happening again in this story. This is a Canadian Telechaniomad.

Aboriginal mythology—of smoke-pipe carriers who do coun-selling services for the village, and the animism that sees spirits in unbreathing things—informs the story on another level. In the foreground, material—real animals, real humans, real steel, real rock—form the hard outside of the story.

The mythical apparatus has fracked into the meaning beds of narrative. The characters seem to rise up, bidden by a desire to access pockets of significance. No classically trained classicist, the author entertained references to mythological stories at his own peril.

Acknowledgments

I would like to thank the gracious all who read portions of this text at various stages of creation and gave me vital feedback, including Jacqueline Holler, Rob Budde, Gary Barwin, Kevin Hutchings, Liz Albl, Noah Campbell, and of course my courageous and scrupulous editor, Malcolm Sutton.

I would also like to acknowledge two pieces of art that appeared, in one case, and influenced, in another, two scenes. *Sour Gas Escape Pod* by Karl Mattson and *Sky Canoe* by Phil Morrison and Al Rempel were both ekphrastic influences. Thank you for the inspiration, and I will leave to the discerning reader to note where this influence is expressed.

We live on a continent where writers are generally free to say what they want, and through the cacophony of expression comes community-wide expression, which is a mending force. So, a final thanks to all my ancestors who stood up for freedom of expression.

Colophon

Distributed in Canada by the Literary Press Group:
www.lpg.ca

Distributed in the United States by Small Press Distribution:
www.spdbooks.org

Shop online at www.bookthug.ca

BOOK
PRODUCTION
WAR ECONOMY
STANDARD

Edited for the press by Malcolm Sutton
Copy edited by Ruth Zuchter
Designed by Malcolm Sutton
Typeset in Nexus Serif, Portrait Text and Source Sans